MÜLLER'S METHOD

Robert Wexelblatt

ISBN: 978-93-6354-337-9

First Edition: 2025
Rs. 200/-

Cyberwit.net
HIG 45 Kaushambi Kunj, Kalindipuram
Allahabad - 211011 (U.P.) India
http://www.cyberwit.net
Tel: +(91) 9415091004
E-mail: info@cyberwit.net

Printed at Repro India Limited.

Acknowledgments

“Müller’s Method” first appeared in *The Literary Review*

“Unwanted Stories of a Zalp” first appeared in *First Intensity*

“Petite Suite Internationale” first appeared in *BlazeVOX*

“Petite Suite Ordinateur” first appeared in *Chiron Review*

“Petite Suite Onirique” and “Hsi-wei and the Mogwai” first appeared in *Modern Literature*

“Lost City” first appeared in *Lowestoft Chronicle*

“Clockwork Orange at Haydn University” first appeared in *Offcourse Literary Journal*

“One-Hit Wonder” first appeared in *Taj Mahal Review*

“March 5, 1953” first appeared in *Cleaver Magazine*

“Falling” first appeared in *Verdad*

Cover illustration: Edvard Munch, *Portrait of Consul Christen Sandberg*, 1901

Contents

Müller's Method

Der Philosoph behandelt eine Frage; wie eine Krankheit.

- Ludwig Wittgenstein

One

Hermann Paulus Müller's contributions to several fields have received, very likely, every bit as much recognition as they deserve. In fact, I would not be composing this account of one of his more bizarre activities were it not for the present controversy in what is, so to speak, the wrong field, and for which, though no one but myself knows it, Müller bears the responsibility. Even so, I think I would be content to remain silently amused if it were not for a niggling professional scruple about authenticity. My stint as a museum curator in the early 1950s—short and sweet as it was—has left me with a heightened sensitivity to every kind of swindle, intentional or otherwise. And a swindle is what this forthcoming German edition of Epictetus' *Encheiridion* is, only the confidence-artist responsible for it has been dead nearly forty years.

I am an Englishman and came to know Herman Müller while I was living in Vienna during most of 1923 and half of 1924. We encountered each other at both informal and professional gatherings, for the intellectuals of post-war Vienna lived in one another's pockets. This was not a purely social phenomenon; it was more the consequence of what I consider a lamentable absence of professionalism. Perhaps it also had something to do with the radical surgery on their Empire. In any case, the Viennese I met all struck me as inveterate dabblers and among them none seemed more promiscuously dilettantish than Hermann Paulus Müller.

Müller's background was upper middle-class. His father had, I gathered, accumulated a small fortune during the years just before 1914, and Müller received a first-rate education. It was rumored, incidentally, that he was "at least half-Jewish," a typically Viennese idiom. Müller was trained as an engineer, though he hadn't much understanding of structural physics judging by an exchange I overheard between him and a disciple of the architect Walter Gropius. Nevertheless, before the war he had published a few minor papers on physics, or perhaps it was mechanics. I suppose it was on the strength of those articles that he wormed his way into the Vienna Circle. I recall someone showing me a slim book of verse Müller had published during the war, and a musical friend once played for me two piano pieces written by Müller. It was said that he had inherited from his father a fuzzy but profitable tie to the Bohemian steel industry and that he had picked up a medical degree somewhere or other. Müller had the reputation of a witty and accomplished man, one of those Schnitzlerian bachelors who are said to "live" at the Café Centrale. When I met him in 1923, he was turning his omnidextrous hand to psychiatry, the latest fad.

I was in Vienna to carry out some research on imperial history. I went to the libraries, of course, but also frequented the museums. I acquired the reputation of an art critic and was often included in conversations on matters aesthetic as well as political. Here I found Müller to be a man of spotty scholarship, uneven taste, and outrageous opinions. I really believe, for instance, that he would have viewed with positive relish the total shambles the art world has been in since 1945. I cannot recall that Müller and I ever agreed on anything; however, I admit that he always treated me cordially and, without actually deferring to my superior knowledge, not without respect. More than once, I felt that it was his wish to impress me, though I find it hard to imagine why, unless he had a case of Anglophilia. Were it not for his desire to earn my esteem, I probably would not hold the key to this *Encheiridion* affair.

Two

All this happened one night in November 1923. I can still remember precisely that evening's conversation, especially certain remarks made by Müller himself. Several of us, including Müller, had attended a racy cabaret performance earlier in the evening after which we retired to somebody's bachelor quarters. The discussion proved as lively as the show.

Motte, a surgeon, a conservative married man, wished to examine the cabaret sociologically. He explained that the comparatively high standard public morality of antebellum days had created a class of *hetaera* which, after restrictions of decency evaporated, had taken to the stage.

A mathematician whose name I've forgotten, demurred. He focused on the contemporary cabaret as a positive cultural phenomenon, a sign of the reinvigoration of an exhausted Europe by a vital Africa via American jazz. He also offered some comments on certain Cubist paintings he had seen on a recent trip to Paris. He asserted, not without insight as it turns out, that these pictures must have been done under the influence of African mask-sculpture. This led to a heated exchange with Motte, who insisted that cabarets and Cubism and jazz and anything American were all proof of the decadence of Christendom.

Müller took a psychological view of the cabarets and what went on in them. "Of course," he said, "the whole thing is a form of imaginary debauchery, and in that there is certainly nothing novel. A great portion of popular culture has always been just that or, if you prefer, a restorative outlet for natural fantasy and libidinousness. Precisely the same words as Motte is using were said a century ago about the waltz-mania. But it isn't just a matter confined to our city; the same things are true of the moving pictures or even," he turned ingratiatingly to me, "the renowned music halls of London."

I remember that as the discussion continued, the others tried to draw Müller out on the subject. It irritated me to see how these men, whose minds were at least as good as his, had gotten into the habit of deferring to him.

Müller, looking satisfied, lit up a cigar and commenced to pontificate. "The transaction is two-fold. The women on the stage, in addition to their pay, receive pleasant sensations from exposing themselves while the men in the audience receive a comparable thrill from observing them. I know I did, anyway." Small pause for comradely laughter. "Now, all this, of course, occurs without touching, without any threat. The enjoyment is not only *of* an illusion but also because what is happening *is* an illusion. Still, what is more interesting to me—and I wonder if any of you noticed them?—is the behavior of the women in the audience. I counted half a dozen of them. When they thought nobody was watching them, these women looked at what was going on even more keenly than you, Dr. Motte! Also, while the men were focused on the stage, these women took in the men who watched as well. I believe that they were the only ones who took it all seriously, the only ones for whom the cabaret was a real revelation—or perhaps I should say a revelation of reality."

There was a hiatus during which no one decided to take up Müller's point. At last Motte rather petulantly offered the following: "But don't you think that sex should be what holds society together and not what tears it apart?"

Müller smiled. "Well, Motte, I think that under some conditions sex can hold *two* people together, but I fear that sexual motivations tend toward a general social dissociation. Think back to your own puberty. Wasn't it a battle between hormones and culture?"

"Really, Müller. I don't see how you can make sexuality out to be anti-social," somebody objected.

"I didn't say it was. It's only another condition of normal life. But sexuality can itself become an expression of anti-sociality, and very frequently is just that. It's astonishing that so many of the people I have been seeing lately—I mean professionally—should be sexually disordered. One might almost think that, since society is ultimately nothing more than the people in it, that, as Doctor Professor Freud suggested many years ago, sex is *the* problem."

"If sex is the problem, then what's the cure?" I asked facetiously.

"Mr. Sterling has, as usual, asked the most difficult question," said Müller then, instead of replying, laughed, exacerbating my annoyance.

"No, really, Müller," said Motte. "What do you do to cure the poor souls that come to you? You never tell us about it. Or don't you cure them at all?"

"I shouldn't tell you: first, because the people who come to me are not at all 'poor souls'—in fact, they are frequently indescribably rich ones; second, because of professional ethics. All my patients are assured of confidentiality as, I trust, are yours, Dr. Motte."

"Oh, get off it. Surely you can give us a case-study or two without names," urged Augenblick, a chemist who had produced some respectable poems. "Your Freud has published several of them."

"That must be because they were worth publishing. The most I can offer at the moment is gossip, and, though I imagine it's for the sake of gossip that people read case-studies, I'll do you gentlemen the honor of presuming you more high-minded. Besides, my method is not yet firm and my data are slight."

After this, the conversation began to melt then dissipate. I was engaged in conversation by Motte who wanted to discuss some event from the time of Empress Maria-Theresa, and Müller talked investments with two men who drew him aside and seemed keen on whatever advice he gave them.

When the gathering finally broke up, Müller and I went off together. It was unavoidable as we were headed in the same direction.

"How about a nightcap at the Centrale?" he suggested, making a point of using the English word "nightcap."

I checked my watch. It was late and I hesitated, but then agreed. Perhaps it was "nightcap" that got me.

In those days, the Café Centrale was never closed and never empty. Its miniature marble-topped tables awaited elbows at every hour. All sorts of people frequented the place and, owing to the housing shortage, I suspect some of the customers who had been wiped out by the post-war inflation might be said to have had their domiciles there. For the price of a coffee, a small schnapps, or torte, one could sit for hours, read the latest newspapers, gossip, or merely enjoy the warmth and light. It always seemed to me characteristic of the city that such an apparently pleasant tradition as café-sitting should be related to such unpleasant facts as worthless currency and an endemic scarcity of flats.

As we seated ourselves, I remarked on this to Müller, who smiled.

"You're very perceptive," he said, "and yet isn't the really essential thing that necessity has been turned into even a little bit of a virtue. Or is there no shortage of affordable flats in London?"

I shrugged.

"But let's talk about something else," he said with that energetic relish of his, as though clearing space for a whole night of conversation. "Tell me frankly, Sterling, what's your opinion of psychoanalysis?"

"Well, to tell you the truth, I think it's a lot of hokum," I said stoutly.

"Hokum?"

"Humbug. Nonsense."

"Oh, really? Well, no doubt, as an Englishman, you're a stolid empiricist and natural skeptic."

"I'm certainly a skeptic about Freud, but not only because my passport happens to be navy blue. I agree with what your countryman Kraus said about it."

"Ach, you must mean Karl's famous *bon mot*—that psychoanalysis is the disease for which it pretends to be the cure? Yes, many people enjoyed that one, even those who only put it down to what some fool said when psychoanalyzing Kraus. For myself, I think the remark a penetrating one."

"You do? Then why have you taken to playing at psychoanalysis yourself?"

"Playing at it? But for me, analysis is no toy, even when it is played with. There's no doubt that play can be of great efficacy in analysis. You see the distinction?"

"Not really. Since you've already declined to say what it is you do, I can't very well judge what you're talking about, can I?"

Müller sipped his schnapps before resuming more volubly and on what appeared to be an entirely new subject. "When I was a boy, I was told a story about a marvelous old rabbi. It seems the man lived all alone in a small hut just outside a village in Galicia—right in the heart of Jewry. He had a reputation as a sage and people—not only Jews but Christians too—came to him from all over to ask for his guidance. There were many examples of his good advice in the story which I have forgotten. The part I do remember is this: whenever a supplicant came through the door of the hut, he would find the rabbi seated before him at a table on which a huge book lay open. And the moment the supplicant began to relate his tale, the rabbi would interrupt and point down at the open book, saying, 'Ah, I've just been reading about your very case.'"

"And do you also sit before your patients with a bible?"

"In a way," said Müller. "Or rather, I like to have them sit before me."

"Why so opaque? You know, I don't understand you in the least."

"I'm truly sorry to sound so obscure, but as I am myself still only feeling my way in these matters, I find it difficult to speak of them other than obliquely. But look, you said you liked Kraus' dismissal of analysis. So do I, and this is because I take it seriously. Analysis means literally *to break down*, and that is the sense in which I think Kraus was correct. How can a psychological breakdown cure a nervous one? Especially if one is speculative and the other genuine?"

"But that," I objected," is just playing with words. Isn't it rather that by forcing the patient to become aware with what is lowest in himself the disorder is heightened, or even created—just as to pick at even a tiny wound is to risk infection?"

"That's altogether possible. Assuming one exits, the disease may, for all we know, take refuge even more deeply as we attempt to draw it to the surface. As a matter of fact, the method with which I am experimenting has something to do with that contingency. But consider this as well: it is a fundamental principle of analysis that only the patient himself can truly effect a cure, if there is to be a cure at all. The analyst is at the very best a sort of midwife."

"Like Socrates?" I joked.

Müller only smiled and drank down the rest of his schnapps.

Three

In those days, to overcome my inclination to be judgmental and widen the scope of my experience in Vienna, I made it a point not to avoid people I disliked. So, though it was past one in the morning, I accepted Müller's invitation to go with him to the place he called his "institute." He wanted to show me some papers.

As we made our way through the city—a good mile or so—Müller talked continuously, his barrel-like frame exploding this way and that in energetic gestures as he prepared me for the marvels he would produce at his office.

"To begin with, you need to know that my patients are all well-educated males. This has aided my experiment, and even suggested aspects of it; however, I hope to generalize my procedures should they be found effective."

"But I've still no idea what you do with these neurotic degree-holders, Müller. Do you examine their dreams, for instance?"

"No, not after the first or second interview. And even then, only if they have a dream they feel compelled to describe to me. Freud's to blame for people mixing up psychoanalysis with oneiromancy. Dreams might be useful in forming a diagnosis, but I've found that diagnosis is the easiest part of the business, at least for my clients who are all thoughtful people. By the time one of them comes to me, he's invariably formed a diagnosis of his own. The trick is in getting him to divulge it. Once I succeed in that, I've no reason to doubt what he says. I've yet to deal with anybody who is really content to stop at a complaint about some mere symptom or aberration. Though one or two would like to remain silent, they are one and all equipped with a detailed hypothesis when they arrive. Finding out what it is saves a great deal of time. And it's not so surprising. Neurotics are generally gifted with, and suffer from, a high degree of self-consciousness. I would even say self-consciousness is a prerequisite for neurosis."

"Yes, fine. I can see that. But what then? If these men already know what's bothering them, what's your task? Is it just a matter of talking to them like a Dutch uncle."

"Dutch uncle? Oh, you English, such colorful language. Well, you shouldn't assume that what's desired, a cure, can be gotten at directly, like an uncle from Amsterdam. You can't come straight to the point for a number of reasons: first, because in dealing with disturbed minds, the shortest distance between point A and point B is seldom a straight line; second, because there may be no 'point' at all; and third, because a proper therapeutic process requires a special effort on the part of the patient himself. As you put it yourself, analysis in depth sinks the patient down into the quicksand and marshes with which he is already all-too-intimate. Instead of forcing him further into the murk, I try to draw the disorder up into the light of reason. As I see it, analysis is concerned with making the unconscious conscious, rather as a plaster draws out a suppuration. But what's 'surface' and what 'consciousness'? If surface is not simply to be superficiality and consciousness not merely a pointless acceptance of emotional clichés, then it has to involve the best efforts of the mind. The patient must, albeit with assistance, become his own physician. That is why I smiled at your allusion to Socrates at the Centrale—that and for one other reason. Socrates is more than an exemplary pedagogue, philosopher, and martyr of the spirit; he is also an exemplary maieutic analyst. That is why I employed him in my first experiment."

I hadn't been listening very closely to all this, but I did catch the last sentence. "What? You used *Socrates*?"

"I couldn't resist. On the surface, it looked a difficult case, even a hopeless one. The patient's a cousin of a friend of mine, and she referred him to me. I'd even met the man on a few occasions. If I told you his name, I think you might recognize it. Several of his books have been translated into English."

"But what's Socrates got to do with it?"

Müller had come to a stop. "I'll explain inside," he said, pointing up a flight of stone stairs toward the tall green doors of a townhouse. By the light of the streetlamp, I saw a new bronze plaque affixed to the wall. It read *The Institute for Advanced Philosophical Analysis*.

Four

"He was my first case," said Müller through the haze of his cigar smoke. "In fact, it was my friend's description of his plight that first gave me the notion to. . . to 'play at analysis,' as you put it. She was desperate, convinced the fellow was going to kill himself."

Müller's office was an odd one. The floor was covered with a fine red and blue Turkey carpet, the pattern of which was the sole trace of order in the room. Two long walnut tables were heaped up with journals and loose papers; a bookcase along one wall looked positively ragged because of all the books protruding from the shelves. A filing cabinet in one corner had been left with two drawers partially opened. Even the armchairs we occupied had to be cleared of papers, some of which I noticed were in Greek. However, the more I examined this disorder, the more it seemed contrived, as when a stage designer wishes to suggest the study of some absent-minded professor. It made me uncomfortable.

"According to my friend," Müller continued, "her cousin's melancholia had two immediate sources: first, a nephew of whom he had been very fond—as bachelors often are—died of influenza in '21, and then the man himself underwent gallbladder surgery the following year. The operation was a success, but he never made a proper recovery—psychologically, that is. He became morose, turned in on himself, and stopped being productive in his work."

"Then the diagnosis was already provided by your friend?"

"Not at all. What she had to tell me was a long way from being a diagnosis. After all, many people lose nephews and organs without turning suicidal. At most these misfortunes were catalysts. The causes are always inward, and in that sense are never factual, as the patient himself taught me. It was from reading this man's books that I realized the full meaning of the separation between inwardness and facts. As he understood this difference himself, there was no point in talking to him about his nephew or his surgery. His most recent book, which came out more than four years ago, was in the field of language theory. I learned more about my patient's illness from reading that book than I did from his cousin, even though the book was written prior to both his bereavement and his operation."

I looked at my watch. It was ten past two. "I know that you're averse to coming to any point, but, anyway, could I ask what the point of this is—and what it has to do with Socrates?"

He chuckled. "Very well; I'll hurry along, though I do want you to understand as thoroughly as possible, you *especially*. . . . Tell me, Sterling, do you know what solipsism is exactly?"

"Being locked up inside oneself, isn't it?"

"Yes, in a way. It's really a metaphysical position, or end-point. It is, so to say, a way of painting oneself into a corner, or better still, burying oneself alive. Solipsism holds that not only is the self the only source of verifiable data, but the self is actually all that exists. All that exists—imagine it! A desperate position, one without any future."

"And that, I take it, was your diagnosis of this author?"

"In part, yes. But even so I don't think I'd have hit on it without meeting with the man. He explained it all to me at our first session, though not directly and without trying to. All you needed was a good long look at him and to hear a few sentences to see that he was on the verge of losing himself *in* himself."

"You're still being evasive. What did you do for him?"

Müller grinned complacently. "I simply had him write a piece of textual criticism."

"You what?"

"I gave him an assignment—to write a critique of a recently discovered fragment of a lost Platonic dialogue."

"Lost dialogue of Plato? But there was nothing in the press."

Müller waved my comment away. "Sterling, of course I made the thing up myself—as my patient was almost certainly aware. I called it 'a fragment of the *Phaedon*.' I'll give you a copy. I've had several extra ones made. Will you do me the honor to read it now?"

Here then is Müller's first piece of therapeutic forgery, the "very case" at which he pretended to be glancing when the troubled supplicant arrived at the door of his miracle rabbi's hut.

Fragment of the *Phaedon*

. . .but then what of Time?

Socrates: By the way, Phaedon, do you happen to know what time it is now?

Phaedon: Certainly, Socrates. It's just an hour after the meridian.

Socrates: And how do you know that, Phaedon?

Phaedon: Why, by observation of the sun, Socrates.

Socrates: Yes, but wouldn't you agree that observation alone is not sufficient to know the time?

Phaedon: In what respect not sufficient?

Socrates: On, in the usual respect. Without a host of concepts, your observation of the sun's position would have no meaning.

Phaedon: I think I see what you mean. But I don't see how it applies to the problem we were discussing.

Socrates: I didn't say it did. But anyway, let's look more closely at the concepts involved in knowing the time. What would you say they are?

Phaedon: Time, of course, and meridian, and hour.

Socrates: And you would say those three are all?

Phaedon: Unless you can think of another. I cannot.

Socrates: Indeed, I can. But so should you. Let me ask you whether you can think of anything that underlies all those concepts.

Phaedon: No, Socrates.

Socrates: But there *is* something. Can't you guess? No? It is the question I asked you: "What time is it?" Not only did the question summon those concepts to mind, Phaedon, but it provided the outline for their connection. In fact, could we not say that questions underlie all concepts? What is the hour? What is time? What is the meridian? What is an hour? What is—anything?

Phaedon: But Socrates, if, as you have instructed me, those concepts already exist in the immutable world of ideas, then how can such questions underlie them?

Socrates: To begin with, I never instructed you or anyone else in anything. I only asked a few questions. But, leaving that aside, there is no great mystery here, just a little paradox. Tell me, do you remember the story about the oracle regarding myself? How it was said by the god that no Greek is wiser than Socrates? It all happened many years before you were born, but perhaps you heard the account?

Phaedon: Who does not know the story, Socrates?

Socrates: Good. And do you remember also how I reacted when I was told of this oracle? How I sought out all those who were esteemed for wisdom among the Athenians and searched for one who was wiser than me so as to discover the error of the oracle? You see, Phaedon,

I knew that I knew nothing, and I held on to my ignorance as it was the sum of my wisdom.

It is knowing that I know nothing that has made me a gift to the state, a gadfly. That is the real moral of the story. Wisdom is a gift of the gods and, in my case, their gift was my ignorance. A gift must not permit his head to swell up just because he is a gift.

Phaedon (protesting): As you say, all that happened long ago. Perhaps *then* you knew nothing, Socrates, but surely *now* you know much.

Socrates: Why do you say so?

Phaedon: But Socrates, everybody in Greece knows that intellectually you. . .

Socrates: Everybody pretended to know all sorts of things before, but when I questioned them I discovered that they didn't know what they thought they did. Why do you suppose things have changed now?

Phaedon: But Socrates. . .

Socrates: No, Phaedon. Before, they pretended to that they know and now it pleases them to pretend that *I* know. But, as I said, the moral of the story is forever the same.

Phaedon: I am staggered, Socrates. However, I still cannot see how it applies to our present discussion.

Socrates: Come now, Phaedon. You are being disingenuous. The connection is by no means subtle. Even now I know nothing—just as before I did not know the hour until you told me; nor, more importantly, did you.

Phaedon: Then in that sense the inquiry underlies the knowledge?

Socrates: Most certainly. However, that is not quite the point either. Tell me, how did you come to be called Phaedon?

Phaedon: I was named after my great-uncle, the one who fell at Potidaea, where you so distinguished yourself, Socrates.

Socrates: Very well. I knew your great-uncle, a brave man. But tell me how *he* came to be called Phaedon?

Phaedon: I don't know.

Socrates: Isn't it because he had to be called something. It was his birth—that is his existence—which caused the first Phaedon to be so named; and so it was with you too, my young friend.

Phaedon: And so?

Socrates: And so it is with all the concepts, forms, and ideas. They too must be born and named.

Phaedon: I still don't understand you, Socrates. How can the changeless and eternal be born?

Socrates: The eternal is eternal only because it is ceaselessly being born, and therefore named. In this way, it is our ignorance of the ideas that keeps them perpetually alive. Without our ignorant questions, Phaedon, the world. . .

(Here the fragment breaks off)

After I finished reading this little fraud, I lay the pages on my knees.

"I think I see," I began. "If I haven't misunderstood, your method is founded on mixing philosophical problems up with psychological ones. All the same I don't see how this," I held up the pages of the dialogue, "could pull any man out of a suicidal melancholy even if he happened to be a language critic."

Müller examined his cigar, got to his feet, walked to the table, and set what remained of the cigar to hiss out in the bottom of a damp teacup. Having made me wait for his reply, he returned to his armchair, seated himself with a grunt, leaned forward on his broad thighs, and delivered another of his lucubrations.

"Look, Sterling, first of all, bear in mind that the man in question happened to be, not a mere student of language, but a philosopher. Secondly, consider that the only distinction between a philosophical problem and a psychological disorder is the language in which a person feels most at home. Thirdly, as I told you, the point of my method is to raise the unconscious not just to the threshold of brute awareness, but to the highest possible level of consciousness—which *is* philosophy. Fourthly, since the patient must effect his own cure—or adjustment—the analyst's task is to furnish him with some manner of doing so. The analyst must set up an appropriate obstacle course, so to speak. And finally, this patient's melancholia was not and is not 'curable' by any means whatsoever. The I am convinced that the word 'cure' is, when applied to the field of psychoanalysis, a misapplied analogy. Anyway, why should one wish to extirpate a sadness that could yield the kind of oeuvre of which this man has shown himself capable? Even if it were possible, a 'cure' would, I believe, be almost criminal in such a case." All this was delivered with great rapidity, earnestness, and as if read from a text.

"But Müller, if no cure is possible or desirable, then what point is there to your method?"

"Ah, Sterling, you're still concerned with 'points,' then? Well, let's try this: say the aim is to enable the patient to *triumph over* whatever it is that threatens his wellbeing or function. Such a victory is the best that can be hoped for, and I devised my method to enable the patient to do exactly that. In the course of working out his interpretation of the dialogue, the patient *did* in fact arrive at a new conception, a new set of possibilities regarding what amounts to his own situation."

"Was he aware that the situation, the problem, was his?"

"It doesn't matter. He was too busy," said Müller triumphantly. "Don't you see how crucial it is that the *Phaedon* fragment is just a fragment? It forced the man to speculate first on what was 'lost,' on the trajectory of the imaginary dialogue, on what preceded and followed it. But then he had *also* to reconsider the whole history of thought, a history which would seem to him to culminate in his own solipsism. Verstehen-Sie?"

Five

I still have my copies of all three "philosophical fragments" given me that night by Hermann Paulus Müller. I don't doubt that when those gullible Teutons publish them, their "newly discovered" sections of Epictetus' *Encheiridion* will turn out to be identical to one of them. Who knows? Perhaps after the *Anschluss* one of Müller's little therapeutic assignments was picked up and carried off with other spoils to that attic in Tübingen. In any case, I should like to steal a march on the dupes at Vorward Verlag.

Müller described the case for which he produced his bit of the Stoic handbook as a dual problem. A young man had become catatonic during a final examination and was brought out of it with difficulty. When he came to see Müller some weeks after, he described himself as wretchedly torn between the duty to obey his father, who intended him for a military doctor, and his mother, who secretly encouraged him to study music. The compounding difficulty, and the cause of the catatonia, Müller rather clinically called "acute ego-involvement." Apparently, the young man had a history of regarding every mark earned by his schoolwork as a sort of divine judgment on his whole self. "No doubt," Müller said, "the source of that touching piece of Calvinism lies with the authoritarian father, but that was not my concern. Besides, the young fellow had figured that out for himself. As the particular examination at which they boy had frozen would have qualified him for medical college, he was reduced to a state of paralysis."

Müller set him the task of writing commentaries on these "lost additions' to the fifty-two known sections of Epictetus' Stoic handbook.

Lost sections of the *Encheiridion* of Epictetus

LIII

You do not live without others. You are not sealed in a bag of skin. You are a son, a brother, a husband, a friend, a citizen. Duties may be discovered by considering these relations because all relations, whether natural or acquired, determine duties. The reverse is no less true; that is, every duty determines a relation. It is your duty to give aid to one who is in need and, by helping him, you form a relation, though you may never have seen the poor soul before. Those who would withdraw into their so-called Gardens desire to evade the role ordained for them by nature, to ignore its imperatives; but an impious life lived in defiance of nature is one which can never yield true happiness.

LIV

How far one should go to fulfill one's duty? Since our existence can have no purpose other than the fulfilment of obligations, the limit of your duty is never the extent of your inclination to carry it out but rather running up against the boundary of another duty. Assume that your brother has been condemned to the galleys but can escape if you agree to take his place. To do this for your brother appears virtuous. But consider that your brother is unenlightened and a thief. Think of your wife, your children, your parents who depend on you to be the pillar of their old age. Were you to take your brother's place in the galleys, what would become of these duties? Could your brother be depended on to care for your family, his parents? The limit of fraternal duty is the filial. And should you be called to defend the city, what then? Just as filial obligation is greater than the fraternal, so civic duty overrides the filial. All apparent conflicts between duties can be resolved by a good will and right reason.

LV

Always remember that we do not care for what we cannot control merely to avoid the risk of unhappiness, but so that we should fulfill our duties and thereby become happy by making our will conform to nature. Remember also that what is beyond your control may be in the power of another so that what is indifferent to you may be his obligation. If you are on trial you may at most prefer a just judgment; however, should you be the magistrate you must care that all your judgments are just in so far as the evidence is available to you. You must care and do so passionately. This passionate caring is common to the instructed and the uninstructed. The difference is that the latter know what to care about and what not to. For the former, unhappiness and dereliction of duty frequently originate in a too lively imagination. The prisoner imagines himself to be the judge, while the judge imagines himself to be a god. In the same way, a son will think himself to be his father and a wife her husband. Those who go about saying 'Oh, if only I were he' make themselves miserable and have no understanding of virtue.

LVI

Were it not for the state, all men would be equal, but they would be equal as stones are. For me, to live in the State is as natural as for ants to live in an antheap.

LVII

Everything depends on how a thing is grasped and never on the thing itself. A bucket is good for drawing water but not if it is carried upside down. If you should think yourself injured by others or by fate, consider that your sense of injury is like carrying a bucket upside down.

LVIII

Many who are just beginning to be instructed resist, complaining that their duties cannot be reconciled and that this proves the worthlessness of philosophy. We find this confusion both reprehensible and absurd. Are not all duties given by nature? And is not an unnatural duty no duty at all? Well then, nature cannot assign us duties that contradict each other any more than nature permits a man to be the father of his own father. Therefore, if you examine your duties giving no regard to personal inclination, the conflicts will invariably evaporate. There are no conflicts between duties, only between virtue and desire.

LVIX

What are human beings? In our essence, we are reason and will; we are not accident. Wealth, eloquence, good family, public honors, physical strength, a pleasing appearance—all these are accidents, even if we exert ourselves to achieve them. Remember that it is characteristic of the uninstructed to weigh an individual by what *happens* to be true of him, of the instructed in terms of what he *causes* to be true. If a person is wealthy or wellborn, say only that he has riches and distinguished relatives, neither more nor less. But as to what he is in himself, reserve judgment until you have removed the blanket of accidents in which every one of us is swaddled.

(End of fragment)

Six

In order that this account might be both definitive and exhaustive, I come now to the final specimen Müller gave me of his method. I call it final not only because it happened to be the last one Müller explained to me that night but also because, soon after, Müller let it be known that he had given up his experiment in psychoanalysis and that he had no intention of publishing his results. The reason for this sudden surrender I had not much difficulty in guessing, but I will reserve my surmise for later.

Müller described his patient as a thirty-six-year-old unmarried attorney. The man lived with his mother and two aunts in a five-room apartment. He had lived there with these women all his life, his father having died when he was four years old. According to Müller, it was a classic instance of female domination. The man was brought to Müller by a mutual friend. He had been at law school with the patient and said he could no longer stand by and watch the further ruination of his friend's life. The patient himself was a contrast to his compassionate and blunt classmate. Müller said that at that first meeting he was passive, soft-spoken, timid, almost prissy. He said little and, though obviously fearful of appearing rude, managed to make it plain that he had come only to please his friend.

Müller's account of his strategy was given with his usual satisfaction. He had managed to reassure the man and elicit his promise to return on another day, without the well-meaning but intimidating friend. There was some trouble in arranging a time when both were free. Müller suggested the following Sunday morning and was, at first, surprised by the man's almost terrified refusal to come on the Sabbath. Another time was fixed.

"Everything is working out very well," said Müller complacently, for their second meeting had occurred that very afternoon. "We actually talked about philosophy the whole time. It turns out he is a great admirer of Kant. He's read it all, even the whole of *The Critique of Pure Reason*. Now just see what I prepared for him!"

I didn't read the "final fragment" then. It was close on four in the morning, and I was too drowsy. So, I took all three texts and, promising to read the last of them, thanked him for a stimulating evening and excused myself. Müller expressed regret. He seemed, if anything, more energetic than he had earlier. The hectic was already burning on his cheeks. It was then that I noticed that flush through a mist of sleepiness and thought to wonder why he had told me everything. After all, I had heard him refuse even a cursory account of his method to his close friends of which I was hardly one.

"One last thing," I said as I rose to leave.

"Yes?"

"Why have you been telling me all this? Why me when you wouldn't tell the others?"

"Why?. . . Tell me, Sterling, do you recall what I said to them about the women at the cabaret, the ones in the audience?"

"Yes, I think so. You said that they were the only ones who took what was happening seriously."

"That's it. They took it seriously because only for them were the performers revealing something of reality. Well, that has been my intention tonight—to reveal this to somebody from the outside whose skepticism and hostility will keep him free of illusions. *Gute Nacht*, Herr Sterling."

I was too weary to protest this cryptic explanation or deny my antipathy and I left.

For several days thereafter I was busy and forgot about the third fragment. I might have forgotten it even longer were it not for a particularly atrocious story appearing in the Monday edition of the *Wiener Zeitung*.

A shocking crime had occurred the day before, right in Saint Stephen's Cathedral. At the conclusion of the Mass, a man had leapt up with a pistol and, before the congregation could overpower him, shot dead the three women kneeling beside him in the pew. According to the paper, the women were the murderer's mother and two aunts.

With a premonition of what I would find, I left the café where I had been reading the journal, returned to my lodgings, rifled through the pockets of my overcoat, and found, along with "Plato" and "Epictetus," the following:

A passage excluded from Nietzsche's *The Antichrist*

Among Kant's many mistakes was regarding man as an end-in-himself. This was not an error in logic so much as a sign of unthinking philanthropy, a crippled imagination and, in that sense, a decaying logic. "If men are not ends-in-themselves, then what is?" asks the good Professor. Of course, he intends this as a rhetorical question, never thinking to put the underlying interrogatories: Why must *anything* be an end-in-itself? Can we think of an "end" which transcends man in general, man *en-masse*? These two questions are precisely those which ought to concern us now that we are at last free to think in earnest, to think like the hammers our time demands.

I wrote that there was a failure of imagination in Kant. But this refers to imagination of only one sort, the good sort, which reflects the facts—for he shares with Christianity (those Pietistic parents of his!) a second kind of imagination, the nefarious, Semitic kind, which is reflective of nothing but the wish to escape the facts, all facts. We have already laid out those respects in which Christianity is a tissue of imaginary causes, beings, teleology, and psychology—a fictional world that does not at all mirror reality but rather sets itself up over against it for the reassurance of the feeble *animo timidum et aequos*. And this is the creature who is an "end-in-himself"?

If pity is the external form of this perversion, then surely guilt is its inward infection and desiccating agent. Pity and guilt serve the same function, though in their separate realms; that is, to side with weakness against strength, to pull down all noble and natural impulses as a tribe of pygmies might a bull elephant. As pity runs counter to and obstructs the natural law of selection, so guilt is the principle by which the individual is kept from rising so much as a centimeter above the stagnant herd.

Say a man of our day feels a sudden access of aggression. Say he had been offended and wishes, as is natural, to strike out at the one who has insulted him. If he has anything left in him of the *homo naturalis*, then he will strike. But then the black spider will clutch at his entrails. "Oh no, this violence is a moral failure. I should have turned the other cheek. Why have I descended [sic!] to the level of a beast?" But, as is more likely, our modern man will not strike; for Christianity has so fortified its perverse idea of guilt that the sensation now *precedes* the act it was once meant to reprobate. And so, a Christian man will feel guilt *for what he has not even done*, but only for momentarily feeling something natural. In this way, he begins through guilt to hate and despise himself. Slave morality not only originates in resentment, it ends in it as well. But exactly what is being resented? Nothing other than nature, than reality. Guilt is willful self-mutilation; indeed, it is a castration of all that remains in us of the genuine, the good, the noble, powerful, natural, and free.

N.B. We might add this to the above: It is a further unclean deformity of Christianity that, while it insists we treat all *others* as ends, it forbids men from regarding *themselves* as ends. Insidiously, this sovereign religion reverses all natural relations, not only between master and slave, but between subject and object. This must be why those apostles and mystics have laid such stress on the verb "to see"—since their visions depend entirely on distortion. Mysticism is a problem in optics rather than metaphysics.

All the believer desires then is to be a tool, a means—like a tube of paint to be squeezed out by another's will. One of the vermin crawling around the corpse of the dead God makes a specialty of this phenomenon. This contemptible worm goes by the name of Romantic Love. "Oh, use me!" cries the emasculated man to his castrating beloved. Love now makes one yearn for a charge of dynamite! And how women adore this lie, making their delight the one possible end, making the smooth-limbed, soft-cheeked eunuch her means. Only "she" possesses virtue; that is, the negative virtue of chastity. The vampirish Eros has become a woman—has become Woman. If modern females all wore carving knives at their hips, then we should at least better recognize the wretched state of things as they are today.

Seven

Hermann Paulus Müller is remembered, when he is remembered at all, as a twenty-watt bulb in the bright chandelier of the Vienna Circle. Except possibly for three dead bodies, I think it can be justly said that his work came to nothing.

I saw him twice after the massacre at Saint Stephen's. The first time was at the Café Centrale a week after the event. I was lying in ambush for him. He came in alone, caught sight of me in a mirror turned on his heel, and fled.

The second time was much later on, only a month before I was to leave the city. We saw each other, in, of all places, a crowded tram. It was a furiously snowy afternoon in mid-February. I had just gotten on when I heard my name shouted from the rear of the car.

"Sterling! Look," Müller yelled in English over the noise. "Look at the driver!"

I looked. The driver was crouched over, trying to peer through an ever-narrowing strip of windshield. In a moment he would be entirely blinded. Then quite suddenly the tram jolted to a halt and, when I turned back, Müller was gone.

Unwanted Stories of a Zalp

About an hour after breakfast, I ambled down to the beach where two boys, a decade younger than my humble self, were building a sandcastle. Their method was the traditional one. After experimenting to get the right sand consistency, the little empiricists filled their plastic pails, overturned them, beat on the bottom with plastic shovels, and laid out neat, inverted towers. Then they backed and filled, sculpted, cut out little crenellations and gouged windows with Popsicle sticks, whispering to each other like freemasons. They were thoroughly enamored of their crumbly medieval stronghold. They wanted it to be a perfect thing, there under the blistering sun and cloudless sky. I remembered building sandcastles and such play is, I know, serious business. I also knew that the painstaking construction is equally aimed at destruction, that boys build things up so that they can knock them down. These are the two chief satisfactions available to little boys on a beach.

"It's obvious that Stephen loves being rich. He isn't ashamed of his money."

"That's not what I said. What I said is I think he's disappointed by it. He's like somebody who's bought this red Ferrari, comes out on the first cold morning, and it just won't start. He wouldn't get rid of the thing, but he feels let down."

"Stephen wouldn't buy a Ferrari, sure as hell not a red one. He hates clichés."

"That's not my point."

"Well, if he doesn't like being rich, why's he go on making money?"

"You're not listening to me. For Stephen, making money's like digesting or breathing. Organisms function regardless of the end."

"Come on. You're exaggerating."

"Not really. Stephen just can't help making money. I mean it's all he knows how to do and so he doesn't dare stop. It keeps accumulating. I'll make a prediction. In the end he's going to be crushed under the weight of his millions."

"Ridiculous. He'll just retire early, set up a bunch of trust funds, a philanthropic foundation, get a hospital wing named for himself or something. He'll marry again and he'll travel. It's what guys like Stephen do. Or it's what their second—or third—wives make them do."

"Why *hasn't* Stephen gotten married again?"

"He got burned and he's naturally cautious."

"I don't think so. I think. . . "

My parents enjoy having this kind of conversation about their friends. They are lucky to have a lot of friends because it gives them plenty to talk about. This is a good thing because it keeps them from talking about whether they are happy being married to each other.

My sister and I, though in agreement on many issues and in alliance on others, don't take the same view of our parents' gossiping. Julie has a horror of gossip; it's almost a kind of phobia. She can't bear to be talked about and, superstitiously, assumes that if she so much as listens to gossip about other people then people will gossip about her. She sees the Golden Rule not as a moral ideal but a cosmic force, like gravity and entropy. This is one of the things I love about my sister, one of her quirks. I tend to like people for their idiosyncrasies more than their virtues, in Julie's case, her good looks, empathy, and skill with algebra. Gossip Julie considers a punishment, a wound in the social life she otherwise likes just fine. I, on the other hand, who fly below everyone's radar and engage in as little social life as possible, look at gossip as a reward. It's compensation for humankind's being a social species and for its division of labor. I find particularly absorbing the occasions when my mother speculates, analyzes, and opines about people about the age of Julie and me. Dad's a reactionary gossip and wouldn't be capable of it on his own. Anyway, trans-generational gossip is always interesting. You'd think they'd be more discreet. In fact, Mom's learned to go mum when Julie's around but with me she's careless.

The night before last Julie was out late and slept through breakfast. This is how I got to hear my mother riff on the subject of Susie. Susie's my sister's oldest friend, though by no means her best one. They go back to elementary school so there's a mindless loyalty there. Susie and her parents are also staying here at Kingston Hall Hotel. Her older brother Maury isn't here because he has a job as head of the waterfront at a camp up in Maine. I'd like it if Maury were here because he calls me "sport" and plays catch with me; a couple years ago he even raised the seat on my bike. Susie, on the other hand, has never held me in anything but contempt. "Your little brother's a creep," she's said to Julie more than once. She never uses *brother* without attaching *little* to it, even though I'm Julie's only brother. According to Julie, I'm not only a creep; she's also called me *nerd* and *dork* and *dweeb*. In the world of pre-college education, pretty much any one-syllable word can be turned into an insult so long as it has a hard consonant at the end of it. Anybody can make them up: frip, twink, zalp. Most of the time Julie stands up for me, but not always. Well, I've learned you can't expect too much even of good people, even the ones you happen to love.

Susie's pretty in an obvious, flashy way which she does her best to emphasize with make-up and the sort of clothes that somehow look passable when parents are around and slutty when they aren't. Apart from a bunch of TV shows, her wardrobe, and her hair, Susie's two major interests are boys and boys who sing, which would be only one interest if all the boys she's interested in could sing.

"I think Susie's seeing one of the waiters," Mom says over the orange juice.

"Which one?" Dad wants to know. As usual, I'm invisible.

"I think his name's Fred or Frank or something."

I want to say it's Frank but don't. I hold my breath.

"Why d'you think Susie's seeing *him*?"

"You didn't notice the way she *didn't* look at him at lunch yesterday? I've been thinking about it."

Dad sighs with comprehension but only moderate interest. "Ah, I see."

So did I. As a rule, Susie looks very carefully at boys like Frank. Sometimes I think she even salivates.

"Gert and Sam haven't a clue."

"About the waiter?"

"About *Susie*. Period."

"Or. . . *no* period?" Dad joked wickedly with toast crumbs in the corner of his mouth. I repressed the impulse to say, Hey, your shy, underweight, well-read, newly adolescent son's sitting right here. And I know about periods. Remember me?

Mom smiled indulgently. "You don't think we should worry about her influence on Julie?"

"No, no. Of course not. Julie's a good, level-headed girl. If anything, *she's* a good influence on Susie."

Dad has his dogmas, especially where Julie's concerned. I sympathize with him. Not only is primogeniture owed some deference, but I share his good opinion of my sister. But Julie as brake drum, as Susie's chastity belt? Maybe, I suppose. On the other hand, Susie as haute suburban tramp—that, as they say, resonated. I mean this is one of those things I knew before I knew it. At my age there are a lot of things you know you knew as soon as you hear them. Mrs. Alter, my geometry teacher, is fond of saying you can learn a lot by keeping your mouth shut. She also thinks that learning is a kind of remembering. Mrs. Alter also told us one day that we knew plane geometry in another life and she's just reminding us. I've found it useful to bear in mind that, no matter what appearances suggest, teachers are neither sane nor crazy, neither friends nor enemies.

"How come you spend so much time alone?" Dad asked me this morning before he left us to drive back to the city and a week of work. It was as if it had just registered on him. I waited to see if he'd add something about it being unhealthy, but all he said was, "Don't you get lonesome?"

I suspect I'm still too young to be lonesome. Grandparents get lonely. Old bachelors and spinsters do too, but not smart-ass, inexperienced boys like me. In fact, I adore being left alone. It's the only thing I ever prayed for.

I had to give Dad a reassuring answer to take with him in the car. "Oh, I'm fine," I said brightly. Then, because he looked unconvinced but eager to be, I embellished. "Yesterday I met a couple guys on the beach, and we messed around with a beach ball. And a Frisbee." I pictured myself leaping in the surf to snag the rising disk as my three new pals—the mesomorphic Athos, Porthos, and Aramis—stood on the shore, cheering my athleticism. You can have as many imaginary friends as you need.

"Well, okay then." It's always prudent to reassure your parents; kids tend to forget how anxious they are. Then Dad had an afterthought. "Hey, I know. How about next weekend we go out fishing?"

"On the ocean?"

He nodded in the direction of the beach. "Where else?"

The prospect didn't attract me. I saw myself puking over the side of a pitching boat, trying to keep my footing on a deck awash with blood and dead fish with desperate eyes.

"We'll see," I said, as if I had suggested the trip instead of him, as if I were the dad trying to defer the moment when I'd have to get out of spending a whole day with my son. *We'll see* is a magic incantation. I learned it from my parents. It's a magic phrase to make the visible invisible.

In a way, I really am invisible because so much of my life is out of sight. But what I imagine isn't always my own life ("filled with so many possibilities," as Aunt Rose ardently declared while pinching my cheek on my tenth birthday). By nature, I suppose I'm a what-if sort of thinker. My favorite part of geometry is always the hypothesis. I picture something happening in certain ways and a lot of this hypothetical stuff grows out of listening to my parents. Their gossip is grist to my busy mill. For example, this morning I've been amusing myself thinking about Stephen Bayer, who, I suppose, is the only millionaire we know but, in my mother's opinion, not a happy man.

Suppose Stephen takes his heap of money and buys a whole town, all the homes and woods and offices and meadows, all the stores, streets, and radio stations. The works. It's a beautiful New England town with old trees, big houses, a clapboard town hall, and white Congregational church. The town square is on post cards. The church gives the new owner a big idea. He decides to establish his own religion and, on a vast tract of conservation land, to build a Gothic cathedral. He has to import workers from Europe to work on it because nobody here knows how to go about building Gothic cathedrals. They all watch too much TV. He invites scholars and theologians to a conference at the hotel he now owns and, in an inspiring keynote address, challenges them to devise a new faith, one with all the good stuff of the old ones but none of the bad.

None of that namby-pamby eclecticism, a dash of Zen a hint of Daoism,standard-issue liberal monotheism that's all forgiveness and brotherhood and no brimstone or absurd rules. I want new stories, better than the old ones. I want pithy sayings people can interpret and argue over for centuries. I want rules too, but also rules for breaking the rules. I want nothing sentimental, or cruel, nothing narrow or sadistic, nothing intolerant, but nothing that looks like a New Age gouache either. I want discipline without constraint, realism redeemed by spiritual depth. I want charity and pragmatism.

I don't want a God of orthodontics or vegetarianism; I don't want any shapeless music. I don't want the God of cartoons and condolence cards.

I want the God of sublime unhappiness, isolation, perplexity, the God of joy and mystery, forgiveness and wit. Now get busy.

The builders, scholars, and theologians throw themselves into their work, fully aware that a chance like this turns up once in a millennium. Stephen immerses himself in the work of every group, writing long memos to the scholars and fables for the theologians, submitting detailed drawings of naves, apses, belfries, buttresses, and gargoyles to the architects. Meanwhile, he clears the town of its old residents. It's expensive to be a feudal lord; you can't be soft, or cheap. Though the cost is gigantic, Stephen's making money all the time, hand over fist. He forgets his unhappy marriage, his nasty divorce, his estranged kids. He thinks only of God and Mammon and how he can use one to serve the other. He declares that henceforth only those willing to join his new church will be permitted to live in his township, which he names New Mynydd after an unpronounceable place in Wales that he passed through in his youth and remembers as immemorially ancient, more lovely and greener than cash.

A couple years ago, I was beaten up at school. I'd like to say I gave as good as I got; in fact, I said exactly that to my parents, though I told Julie the truth. I make a point of not lying to Julie and, besides, she'd heard about it anyway. The *casus belli* was obscure. Apparently, this bruiser named Joel Horrocks didn't care for my looks or my books or my grades or, more likely, he simply found my vulnerability impossible to resist. He began with a few prosaic insults accompanied by the customary chest-pushing. This was dangerous because at the time we happened to be on the top of the stands in the gym, twenty feet above the hardwood. I had to think about a lot at once: not backing up too much, not falling, not looking scared, not saying the wrong thing, not embarrassing myself in front of the dozen kids who gathered like crows around a squashed squirrel. To my credit, I didn't try to weasel out with humor. I pushed back. Unfortunately, I did it too well. I caught Joel by surprise, and he fell down a couple of steps. My heart skipped a beat in triumph and terror. I think his eyes turned red. I could see myself through them.

"I'll teach you to push *me*," he growled as he rose up like a grizzly.

"Looks like I already know how," I was unable to resist mumbling. This was a capital mistake, even worse than my lucky shove. The thing you have to know about born anti-heroes is that they all yearn to be heroes. It's a prerequisite, like plane geometry. But an anti-hero's not supposed to act on heroic impulses.

Joel did teach me something. He taught me to cultivate the cunning you only get from solitude.

A rainy day at last. After lunch, Julie went up to her room to read. She reads almost as much as I do which is remarkable because, unlike me, she also does lots of other things.

I knocked softly, in case she had fallen asleep.

She knew it was me. "You can come in."

Julie was lying with her head at the foot of the bed, the big blue complete Shakespeare propped against her thighs, two pillows under her head, another under her bare feet.

"More Shakespeare?"

"I told you. Mr. Rabinowitz gave me a reading list."

"Rabinowitz gave *every*body a reading list. You think anybody else is bothering?"

She laid Shakespeare aside. "You're a fine one to talk. What is it now? Dostoyevsky? Thomas Mann? Thomas *Wolfe*?"

"I like fat books. So sue me." I gulped at the clumsy segue. "And speaking of Sue—is Susie fooling around with that waiter, Frank?"

Julie crossed her arms in the universal symbol for intransigence. As if she'd tell me.

"Okay," I said. "Fair enough. But you know Mom's worried she might be corrupting you. Said so yesterday morning. Dad refused to hear of it, of course. He thinks you'll uncorrupt Susie."

My sister was indignant, which I enjoyed; but she blushed, which I didn't.

I sat on the edge of her bed. "Which one you reading?"

"*Much Ado*."

"Ah, let's see." I grabbed the book and read some first-rate Benedick. 'I will fetch you a tooth picker now from the furthest inch of Asia; bring you the length of Prester John's foot, fetch you a hair off the great Cham's beard, do you any embassage to the Pigmies, rather than hold three words conference with this harpy.' Will could really tickle them ivories, couldn't he?"

"You think Susie's a *harpy*?"

"Susie? But that's *Beatrice*. And Benedick's *nuts* about Beatrice."

"I'd tell you to go tease somebody your own age if I could only figure out what it is."

"Jule?"

"Yeah?"

"What do *you* think of Susie?"

Silence.

"Okay. Let's talk about comedy then."

"You can talk, then I want to get back to the play."

"As I see it, it's a matter of biology. I mean as tragedy is to death comedy is to sex. Sex is what makes happiness an ending. Triumph of life."

She twisted on the bed. "Oh, so you've been thinking about sex?"

"Five times every waking minute, according to the latest research."

Julie lets me check out her dates. She relies on my judgment. We have a twenty-point scale and, so far, I haven't given anybody above an eight. I take the responsibility seriously. I'd give Maury at least a fourteen if he got around to asking Julie out.

I think dating's comical because it's about sex too. In sex, as in comedies, people are undignified, mechanical, limited, sympathetic, and, if it goes well, everybody gets lucky. The action needs intrigue, obstacles, revelation, but really it's all aimed at coupling, isn't it—or delaying it just long enough. Comedy isn't any more artificial than tragedy; it just feels like it is. Comedy appears to be contrived, unnatural; but that's ironic, since it's about what nature uses to get what it wants. Copulation, I mean.

Puberty, as Joel says, "really sucks". Girls say it twice—really *really* sucks. Puberty's a frip, a geek, a zalp. To this favor must we come. Thus doth nature make werewolves of us all.

Here's how I'd make a comedy. First, you have three guys. Let's say one's a narcoleptic, another's into making money, and the third's an ascetic trying to kill off his libido. That's Scene One. Scene Two: three females. One's a romantic, another's a bluestocking, and the third's a fantasist. You get all six of them in the same place at the same time and add some blocking characters: fathers, mothers, dukes, uncles, or aunts—maybe even some little brothers. Then it's a matter of arranging intrigues and wrongheaded match-ups. Then, in the end, you square everybody away. The narcoleptic's woken up by the fantasist and the fantasist calms down; the greedy bastard learns about love from the romantic who learns to be more practical from him, while the bluestocking dumps her books to smooch with the ascetic, whose libido dormant leaps back to life. They're all cured, all balanced. A miracle. Three quick weddings then down comes the curtain, which is to say the bedroom shade.

Sunny today, resort weather. I spied on Julie and Susie this afternoon, down by the beach. Well, *spied* is too strong a word; it implies intention and stealth. Let's just say I checked them out. Susie especially. I wanted to see if she'd lie on her stomach and untie the top of her bikini, which she did after about five minutes. *A swallow'd bait on purpose laid to make the taker mad.* (Will can sing about anything.) All curves, like Grushenka, and, like any Russian siren, liable to broaden in a few years.

Next year Julie's going to be a senior. After that, she'll be off to college where I can't watch over her, vet her suitors. I expect she'll major in math. That should scare off some of the shallower types. I hope she goes for some guy who can appreciate her brain, a Benedick who'll love and spar by turns. Someone like Maury.

Julie didn't have Shakespeare with her on the beach. Maybe you can write poetry on a beach—Matthew Arnold did it—but who reads the stuff there? Susie had a paperback novel with her, one of those things with suggestive covers and tin-foil covers. Julie had a paperback, too. I checked it later. It was a collection of Katherine Mansfield stories. I felt reassured.

It's not true that you are what you read, only that you are what you read between the ages of fourteen and maybe twenty-five. I read good books for the same reason other people (e.g., Susie) read bad ones—to escape. But the difference is that the good ones don't let you escape, not for long. I'm in Russia with Raskolnikov, I'm up the Congo with Marlow, I'm in Dublin with Daedalus, in Venice with Aschenbach, in Spain with Jake, in Normandy with Emma, in eternity with K. Sure, but I'm still here, too. More here than ever. I forget myself but at the same time, page by page, in accord with Mrs. Alter's theory, I remember myself, or I acquire a self to recollect.

I read classics. It's more a matter of taste than precociousness. Taste has given me the kind of swollen vocabulary I can't use at school. But I have to be honest. My impulse is the same as that of the housewife with her Regency romances, the lab assistant with his stack of sci fi, the retiree with her tower of Agatha Christies. We all want out of the banality. We all hate commercials.

Julie's good at math and I'm not. Maybe that's why she's tied to the world while I feel like I'm barely holding on by my fingernails.

I took a good long look at Susie, at that eloquent curve from nape over scapulae down to small of the back up over buttocks down thighs and calves to exquisite ankles. Maybe Julie could graph it, find the equations, but Susie's body made me think of a cello. Someday it'll be the other way around, no doubt. I'll be at a recital and think of Susie in her prime, prone on the beach.

Now Susie's story is a doozy, even lacking a finish. But, except for the comedy, none my stories have proper endings.

I imagine Susie and Frank get hitched during her sophomore year. She drops out with relief. She wasn't learning anything anyway. Her parents have to swallow hard and Maury's all stolid disapproval, but what can they do? She's six months pregnant. Julie is maid-of-honor at the wedding; that I'm not invited goes without saying. The marriage lasts all of about a year.

But that's just back story, the stuff you imagine but leave out, author's scaffolding.

I picture a nice, well-maintained suburb. It's the kind where people fuss over their lawns and have kids and make the town put in speed bumps and buy minivans to bump over them. It's a Saturday morning in April.

A young woman, good looking, only a little plump, goes from door to door.

"Excuse me," she says with a brilliant smile. "Is there anyone here who'd like to have sex with me? Male or female, either's fine. No? You're absolutely sure? You wouldn't care to think about it for a few minutes, over coffee, say? Well, thanks for your time anyway. Oh, may I leave my phone number for your husband?"

A couple observations: a) it's easier to make happy people feel guilty than miserable ones; b) adults remember good times with less feeling than bad ones. Why? a) Maybe unhappy people don't have to feel guilty for being happy whereas happy people are, so to speak, already set up to feeling guilty about it. b) In bad times, life's more vivid and so more memorable, cherishable.

Julie feels guilty at the drop of a reproach but Mom, who's more dissatisfied with her life, just absorbs blame with a shrug. "I've got broad shoulders," she likes to say. When I think back on the day Mr. Galheim accused me of plagiarizing the first essay I wrote for him ("Searing Innocents: Huck Finn and Holden Caulfield," ten pages) I almost feel fond of my younger self. Searing Innocents—or innocence. I'm even pleased to recall Galheim, if only because of his face when I produced my rough draft and a few additional *aperçus*. The poor old guy. It was sixth grade and all he'd asked for was two pages of comparison and contrast. I was happy-go-lucky in sixth grade and guilt is just what I didn't feel when I was accused, only the resentment of injustice, which felt exhilarating and demoralizing at the same time. To this day I can't bear to watch frame-up movies. But I do watch other things.

For instance, last night there was a documentary on about the Battle of the Bulge. Mom wanted to watch sit-coms and Julie was out at a movie with Susie, one of those summer movies aimed at fourteen-year-olds-of-all-ages.

"Please, Mom," I begged. "If Dad were here, *he'd* watch it."

"You got that right. Hitler and the Battle of Britain and D-Day and Pearl Harbor and Midway—he can't get enough of them. But your father isn't here."

"But he'll be back tomorrow. I'll tell him about watching it and we'll bond. Bonding with your father's extremely important at my age."

She looked at me sharply. Why is it my parents always seem to be seeing me for the first time?

"Okay, then. I have to phone Aunt Rose anyway. Enjoy the war."

Dad was born during the Battle of the Bulge, during the first week, on December 19, 1944. At some point when he was growing up, he must have learned this. Once I asked him about his fascination with the Second World War.

"To us, it wasn't yet ancient history," he said, "like it is for you." I noticed he said "us" and figured that it was a generational thing, that his whole generation of little boys were caught up in the war. "But to our parents it was only ten years ago. That's nothing. The war supplied our toys, our games. There was army surplus stuff all over the place. I had a canteen, one of my friends had a Japanese bayonet and this black SS helmet with a bullet hole in it. You built models of the fighter planes, read the stories. You watched *Victory at Sea* with your family every Sunday afternoon. Maybe it was all history, but it was nearby too."

Dad has a lot of books about the warplanes of the era. Why is it that obsolete weapons look so beautiful? Is it just because the threat's gone?

I watched the whole documentary. Two hours of it. Hitler's last gamble was so stupid and obviously futile, and yet all the Germans went along with it, veterans, old men, kids just a little older than me, little heads rattling around in shovel helmets. The GIs were so confused, boys too, raw recruits in the spooky forest. The weather was awful. The strategy was simple-minded. For example, I can't understand why Eisenhower didn't use a pincer movement when the attack finally stalled. He just pushed back for a month, a five-week frontal assault that made me think of a foolish man pushing his car out of a snowdrift.

But what interested me most was an interview with a lady from Luxembourg. These days she looks a bit like the old lady who civilizes Babar, but there was a photo of her as a young woman. She had the same long European face but unlined and with the peculiar hair-do of the forties, nearly shoulder length with tight curls. She talked about happening on the Nazi build-up, pretending to be German when they caught her, making her way to the Americans to warn them, being ignored. She talked about huddling with her family in the basement of their farmhouse, about celebrating Christmas smack in the middle of a frozen *Götterdämmerung*. I liked that she spoke unsentimentally when you could see she felt so much.

I don't think sentimentality's ever to be trusted. Feeling isn't good for much, actually. That's one problem with religion, incidentally. Religion, like Supermarine Spitfires and Messerschmidt 109s, starts out as lethally serious and ends up as aesthetic, as ornamental. Sentimentality's what does it.

Dad doesn't know my favorite WWII story. This is it. After the German surrender, an American GI, a young intelligence officer who had been principal oboist in Pittsburgh before the war, learned that the composer Richard Strauss was still alive and holed up in his country house in Garmisch. He went to pay his respects to the depressed octogenarian. Strauss was a Nazi, at most a half-hearted one, and the Americans gave him a pass. This is the same Strauss who wrote the pompous *Ein Heldenleben*, the sophisticated Strauss who wrote *Der Rosenkavalier*. The intelligence officer visits Strauss often to talk of music, not politics. He asked Strauss if he'd ever considered writing an oboe concerto and Strauss bluntly said no. The American went home but only months later learned that Strauss was publishing a final outpouring. The autograph on the score of his oboe concerto reads "1945 - inspired by an American soldier." I heard the piece once. It's pretty jolly.

Today's story: I imagined the thoughts of the children and grandchildren of the survivors on the December day when the church doors were shut.

There's snow everywhere but they call it "just a dusting." It's below freezing but they say there's "just a nip in the air." For civilians who lived through the Battle of the Bulge, every winter is compared to the December when you couldn't step into the forest without tripping over frozen soldiers. They go on about the shell holes spattering the fields as though giants had taken dumps. They can still taste the bread made from sawdust, eating cold turnips. *How can you understand*, they say with the pardonable arrogance of those who have truly suffered. *To you, hunger's just a tickle you feel before sitting down to your poulet rôti.*

Every year between Advent and Christmas the old people meet in the church and stay there from noon until suppertime. Not even the minister is allowed to join them. It's understood. They are there to share with each other the grief and horror of that most terrible winter, to whisper to one another what's not to be spoken of to us, to relive the eight weeks when the fate of Europe was decided outside their parlors, across their fallow fields. People who have gone through something like that, people who have been spun around in the rinse cycle of history, deserve not to be intruded upon. This reunion is solemn and somber, a sacred thing. We keep our voices low, too.

We all thought we knew what went on in the church on those dark December afternoons. We pictured the old folks crying on each other's shoulders, clicking their tongues over lost brothers, husbands, sisters, children. They would again drink snow and hear the whine and crump of 88s, the popping of machine guns and the yells of crazed, terrified soldiers. They would again fail to find words to describe the smells.

We've all seen pictures of the black-and-white battle, the grey tanks and flaming jeeps, the men exhausted and bitten by frost, the bloody avenues between the evergreen. We recognize our Ardennes in these films; and yet, we remind ourselves, the land wasn't ours then; it belonged to the old folks caught in the middle. We're here because they survived, chose life, and repopulated the ruined villages with us.

They had the misfortune to be there for the final battle of all those that had churned up our land since the Hundred Years War, each larger and deadlier than the one before. They were the heirs of Agincourt and Waterloo and the Somme, not us, and so there were no allowances we wouldn't make.

We pitied and respected them. We felt lucky because the war had been so horrible there could never be another. It was as if they had suffered for us, as if they had won the war against both sides and bought us our quiet nights and Christmas trees.

So, it was hardly possible to believe the story told by the Friesant boy. He said he'd been going past the church on his way to his cousins' house when something caught his attention. He stole up to a window that had been stuck open a crack. He couldn't see inside—the window was too high—but what he heard, and he swore to it, was laughter, great peals and howls of laughter.

Julie and I went out to the pool after breakfast. We sat on the empty patio, on the chaises. A deserted pool is melancholy; it felt like the last scene in an Italian film.

"You look glum. What's the matter?"

"I look glum?"

"Morose, depressed. You know, *sad*."

"I don't know. I had a bad dream last night. This morning, actually."

"Really? What was it about?"

"I don't remember much."

She was really interested, almost as interested as in her SAT scores, almost as interested as Susie was in Frank. "Try," she insisted.

"Okay. What I remember's just kind of a feeling. I felt like, I don't know—like somebody who's given up trying to be happy. It was like how I imagine being middle-aged, or dead."

"Where were you?"

"At home. In the dining room."

"The dining room? Was anybody *else* in the dream?"

"Mom and Dad were there."

"What were they doing?"

"Eating dinner. Talking about me as if I weren't there."

"Anybody else?"

"Susie."

"Susie? And did *she* see you?"

"Yep. She was eating chocolate cake. She called me a creep and giggled."

"Wasn't *I* there?"

"No. You were married and living in some place like Oregon."

"Oregon? Really? So, who was I married to?"

"Susie's brother."

"You're making this up."

"Maybe. But dreams are made up too."

"You make up too many things."

"But I still want to be happy someday."

"Of course. Who doesn't?"

"I mean it."

Julie got up and gave me a kiss on the top of my head. "Come here," she said.

She led me over to the side of the still, turquoise pool. Then she pushed me in.

Petite Suite Internationale

1. *La Retraite de Castel Ceriolo – Adagio pour Cor Français et Orchestre Militaire dans les Coulisses, lent, énervé, et équivoque*

The fifty-seven-year-old agricultural worker, Christophe Moulin, had been among the veterans who rallied to Bonaparte's standard after his almost miraculous return from Elba. Like many others, Moulin's feelings about the Emperor were less than whole-hearted; nevertheless, he resented the restored Bourbons' insulting conduct toward not only the remnants of the Grande Armée but the whole of the French population. He despised the émigré rats scrambling back aboard the ship of state with their arrogance and greed sharpened by exile. Together with prisoners of war repatriated from the East, men hardened by combat and deprivation, he joined up for what the literal-minded historians of Europe had taken to calling the War of the Seventh Coalition. Moulin felt a bitter pride in having been there for the Belgian finale. But he had been there at the start as well, in Italy. What he remembered most vividly was not the defeat of 1815 but the glory of 1800, when he was not yet eighteen years older than the new century.

Now Moulin was limping down a road in the Auvergne, getting away from the Coffinhals. He did not consider that he had panicked in the face of the enemy. No, his tactical retreat was, in fact, a victory. The sobbing of his daughter and the ridicule of his son-in-law resounded in his ears as he tossed his bag over his shoulder and set out. As for the children, they were playing with their latest toys and couldn't be bothered to see their grandfather off. He was sorry to leave Juliette but glad to depart.

Moulin had married Juliette's mother, a good Republican maid from the Allier, shortly after the demobilization. They met that autumn when he was hired to pick apples in the orchard of Françoise's uncle. Juliette was born the next summer. It was a difficult delivery and Françoise had never regained her strength. She died in the terrible winter of 1817 when Moulin had struggled to find firewood, food, and work. But he had kept the child alive, and Juliette grew to be so beautiful that even without a dowry she attracted many suitors. Of these, Coffinhal was the one Moulin liked least. He was good-looking, suave, very sure of himself, and in a hurry. He bragged of his plans. For Moulin's taste, the young man was too much in accord with the status-quo with its marriage of political repression and economic laissez-faire; also, he dressed too well. He was full of promises, had already secured a position in one of the new banks popping up everywhere like weeds, and Juliette had fallen in love with him. There had been heated discussions between father and daughter, but Moulin was incapable of denying his daughter anything she truly wanted. He gave in and, at the church in Doyet, gave Juliette away.

Coffinhal had prospered in the bank and still more through shrewd land speculation. He and Juliette had two children and, when they moved into a substantial house in the country between Riom and Mozac, Juliette had begged her father to come live with them.

"We can make you comfortable. Don't you want to see your grandchildren grow up? You're too old to go on doing such heavy work, Papa," she had argued.

"But not old enough to lose my liberty," he had replied like a good revolutionary.

Juliette dismissed this and touched on the real point. "Georges isn't so bad as you think."

"I'm reassured to hear it," Moulin had retorted, and that was the end of the matter until he had mounted Detouches's rotting ladder and broke his leg. Juliette rushed to him. She put her foot down and Moulin consented to stay, but only until he recovered. The look of loving triumph on Juliette's face signified to Moulin that she believed he would never leave.

For a week, Georges Coffinhal behaved toward his father-in-law with courtesy; though his politeness was chilly and forced, it was sufficient to satisfy his wife. Nevertheless, he found it difficult to conceal his annoyance at the attention his wife lavished on the old man. He frowned every time she fetched him a footstool or offered hot chocolate.

Coffinhal like to dominate dinner conversations with a mélange of name-dropping and sums of money. This aggravated Moulin.

"I ran into Portendieu this afternoon. He let me know that the new Marquis d'Anjony—who inherited a fortune including a vineyard in Burgundy—is in want of a new carriage and four matched horses to pull it. I had a word with Castignac and I think I can expect a tidy fee. I might make inquiries about whether the Marquis might be interested in that property in Le Puy with the good view."

Georges Coffinhal christened his son Georges—what else?—and certainly not Christophe. The second child, little Berthe-Marie, was named after his mother. Neither child liked having Moulin in the house and the antipathy was mutual. Georges had two attitudes toward his interloping grandfather who, he'd been told, worked on other people's farms: contempt and fear. The little girl was willful, given to tantrums, disobedient, and precociously vain. Moulin overheard her complain to her mother, "But Maman, he smells so bad!" They were a brace of spoiled children and Moulin did not pretend otherwise.

The tension in the house was just bearable until the afternoon Coffinhal brought home a newly published novel, Stendhal's *Charterhouse of Parma*, and handed it to Moulin at the dinner table.

"Adolphe Bertin gave this to me, though not with much of a recommendation. I read the opening sentence and thought it might appeal to you, Christophe."

This speech he delivered as he did the book, almost with distaste.

"Go ahead," he said with a smirk. "Read the first sentence."

Moulin opened the book.

"No. Read it aloud," Coffinhals insisted.

Juliette, who had always been fond of novels, and had enjoyed *The Red and the Black*, failed to catch her husband's tone. "Oh yes, do, Papa."

Moulin read. "*On 15 May 1796, General Bonaparte made his entry into Milan at the head of a youthful army which but a short time before had crossed the Bridge of Lodi and taught the world that after so many centuries Caesar and Alexander had a successor.*"

"Oh, children!" exclaimed Juliette. "Did you know that your grandfather was in that youthful army?"

Little Georges scoffed like the miniature version of Coffinhals he was.

Berthe-Marie went her brother one better and made her father laugh. "Grandfather was young?"

Moulin looked at his grandchildren severely. "You youngsters have no idea what we were fighting for, do you? Your history lessons say nothing of the First Republic, do they?"

"That's not true," Georges protested. "We know about the guillotine cutting off the heads of all the best people."

"Best people?"

"That's what aristocrat means, grand-père," said Georges condescendingly.

"That's enough," said Juliette.

But it was too late.

"The boy's not wrong," said Coffinhals. "The Revolution was a catastrophe and it led to your upstart Bonaparte who was both quixotic and pernicious."

Your Bonaparte. The pronoun hit like a shell striking a depot.

Without a word, Moulin stood and left the table. Five minutes later, as his son-in-law grumbled, "Let the old Jacobin go," and Juliette tearfully begged him to stay, Moulin threw his portmanteau over his shoulder and was on the road.

His mind left his family behind as quickly behind as his body. Now both were free to go where they wished.

Stendhal's stirring phrase "youthful army" had excited Moulin and, as he shambled into the June twilight, he was transported back to that other June of thirty-nine years before. There had been marching then, too, double-quick on the orders of the man he revered above all others, General Louis Charles Antoine Desaix, the thirty-one-year-old commander whom they'd called "the good aristocrat".

Years before, when his eyesight was better, Moulin had made it a point to find out all he could about the dashing Desaix. He was one of those rare, fiercely republican aristocrats who refused to emigrate. He barely escaped the guillotine and joined the cause, the youthful army. At the age of twenty-four he was already a divisional commander. In June 1800, Napoleon put him at the head of two divisions.

The battle might easily have been lost. Von Melas's surprise attack nearly succeeded. After defeating von Bátorkéz at Montebello, Napoleon, deceived by a double-agent, sent forces to the north and south, including Desaix's divisions. Seeing the French divided, the Austrians launched two assaults on Berthier's position at Marengo. Grasping the situation, Bonaparte moved up his reserve and sent a staff officer off at the gallop to recall Desaix. By mid-afternoon, the French were in full retreat, the Austrians pressing their advantage. Desaix had reached Rivalta when he heard the cannon at Marengo. Taking the initiative, he ordered his men to turn around and march at speed toward the sound. He met the courier on the way.

Moulin recalled how they had arrived late in the day as the Austrians were advancing in triumph. He could still see Desaix on his horse and hear him shout, “There’s yet time to win another battle!” Then he had lowered his saber and led Moulin’s regiment and two others straight at the Austrians’ center. They had stabilized the line so that the trap Napoleon had hastily prepared could be sprung. Ordering musket and cannon fire to create a concealing fog, he loosed the surprise attack of de Kellerman’s cavalry, pushing the Austrians back with huge losses, driving them clear out of Italy.

French casualties were comparatively light yet costly enough. Desaix’s brave words were his last ones in this life.

Bonaparte may have been an egomaniac, but he was never one to overlook the heroic service of his officers. Desaix’s name figures on the Arc de Triomphe and Napoleon personally ordered two monuments erected in his honor. Perhaps it’s fortunate, Moulin thought, that our good aristocrat didn’t live to see his republican ideals betrayed by his commander.

June 14, 1800, he mused, the day I was most alive, the day when, arriving breathless and just in time below the castle of Ceriolo, in a twilight just as soft as this, we fixed our bayonets, took one deep breath, ran shouting toward the astounded Hapsburgers, and secured the Republic.

Now, so many years later, on a plodding, less purposeful trek, Christophe Moulin felt as if his brigade’s desperate march and headlong charge only appeared to have saved the Republic. Instead, he suspected that, though nobody could have anticipated it, in some way the death of men like Desaix foretold the triumph of those like Coffinhals.

2. *Analyse Académique - Duo Contestable à la Manière d’une Parti Perdu pour Violoncelle Ensommeilléet Hautbois Trop Éveillé*

At four-thirty on a Monday afternoon an email chimed into Uwe von Gerstenberg's Inbox. It was an official communication from the Vice Chancellor's office with a request that he click on the link to a questionnaire about student engagement. The message explained that a similar questionnaire had already been sent to students, thanked him in advance for his cooperation, and declared that the data gathered would be of the first importance to the University. The link was not to a University site but to something called Bildungsanalytik, GmbH.

Uwe frowned and clicked on the ink which told him, among other things, precisely how long it would take him to complete the questionnaire. At the bottom of the page, in tiny gray print, inside a lighter gray lozenge, was the word *decline*. Uwe clicked on it and was at once informed that he would be unsubscribed. He then returned to answering anxious emails from two of his students, one gifted, one not, both insecure. An hour later, he left his apartment and walked to Grauber's for early dinner with a friend from graduate school who had phoned the day before to say he would be in town for a conference. Could they get together? The friends both ordered sauerbraten and split a bottle of Trollinger. The conversation being both nostalgic and convivial, they ordered a second bottle.

At six forty-five the following morning, Uwe, not entirely over the wine, was awakened by a well-groomed young man in a blue business suit smiling at him from the foot of his bed.

"Guten Morgen, Dr. von Gerstenberg," said the young man with a little laugh. "Rise and shine."

It is disconcerting to be roused at dawn by a stranger at the foot of one's bed; if he laughs at you as well, it is humiliating.

Groggy, indignant, and vulnerable, Uwe demanded how he had gotten in.

The young man laughed again and held up a key. "This is a university apartment," he explained.

"Who are you?"

The young man gave a rather ironic little bow. "Jürgen Bock."

"But what are you doing here?"

"I'm an employee of Bildungsanalytik, Dr. von Gerstenberg. Perhaps you'll recall declining to respond to our questionnaire at four thirty-seven yesterday afternoon?"

Uwe just stared.

"We would like to know why you made that decision, Dr. von Gerstenberg. May I call you Uwe?" He held up his clipboard and, with yet another little laugh, said, "I feel that I know you very well."

"I declined because declining was an option," grumbled Uwe.

"Yes, to be sure. We always include that choice. But, with respect, you haven't accounted for your decision to use it."

Uwe's mind went back a bit. "Why would you say you know me?"

Grinning, Bock glanced at his clipboard then reeled off a speech *prestissimo*.

"Your Danish great-grandfather, an ironworker, emigrated to Hamburg in October 1899 and married. The family remained in Hamburg and is still there. You were born three weeks prematurely and have two siblings, an older sister, Margarete, and a younger brother, Johannes. Father was a railroad official, Mother a homemaker and avid reader. She introduced you to books and it was reading that sustained you through a rather lonely adolescence. In your sixteenth year alone, you read three novels by Dostoyevsky, two by Thomas Wolfe, one by Albert Camus, and all of *War and Peace*. Back in eighth grade you were three times punished for reading in class and not paying attention to the teacher. At the Gymnasium you excelled with an overall average of 3.87. You earned your undergraduate degree at

Heidelberg *cum laude*. After contemplating a degree in law, which was your father's wish, you switched to German literature. It took you four years to complete your dissertation. Your doctorate was conferred on you by the University of Bonn. You wanted to write a thesis only on Heinrich von Kleist but your advisor, Professor Klugscheiner, insisted you write also about Jean Paul, born Johann Paul Friedrich Richter. You were indifferent to Jean Paul but loved the writer who lived half as long and produced one-tenth as many pages. Klugscheiner insisted on Jean Paul not out of any enthusiasm for his work but because he judged a dissertation including two writers would make you twice as employable, which turned out to be prudent advice."

Another glance at the clipboard and Mock went on.

"You've had three girlfriends in the last six years. None of these relationships lasted less than three or more than thirteen months. You brush your teeth for two minutes, after which your electric toothbrush is programmed to shut itself off, a good habit on which I congratulate you. You favor jeans with a 30-inch inseam and a 32-inch waist, cable-knit sweaters and an old black suit jacket originally purchased for your grandmother's funeral eight and a half years ago. Since securing your appointment here at Freiberg as junior professor you have published seven articles, three reviews, and delivered four conference papers. Last semester, your students gave you, on average, 4.4 out of 5 points on their evaluations. They are in accord in praising your pedagogy; the standard deviation was exceptionally low. Only three criticisms stood out: two didn't care for your haircut and one found you—what was his word?—yes, a little too apodictic in class discussions."

Here Uwe, now fully awake, interrupted Bock's torrent of words.

"Did any of the students say that they learned anything?"

This drew another little laugh. "Well, Uwe, the grades you gave them averaged 3.16, so I presume they did."

"Yet you can't say what, can you?"

"We'd know better had you given them multiple-choice examinations."

Uwe scoffed. "Would true-false questions have been better?"

"Not necessarily better—just simpler. Binary."

Uwe threw off the covers. "Would you mind if I peed and then brushed my teeth for two minutes?"

"Oh, sorry. Thoughtless of me." This time Bock's laugh was apologetic. "Of course. What do you say? Shall I make us some coffee?"

On his way to the bathroom, Uwe said over his shoulder, "Why not? You'll find everything in the kitchen."

"How many cups should I make?" Bock replied through the closed bathroom door.

"Four and three-eighths."

Uwe, finished in the bathroom, pulled on sweatpants and a cable-knit sweater, then went into the kitchen and sat at the oak table that came with the apartment.

Bock was standing by the coffee machine. "Our chief job is not merely gathering data, you know."

"No?"

"It's assessment. That's why your participation is so important. It will be a real contribution. It's why your Chancellor hired us."

Uwe shrugged. "How's it work?"

"You really want to know?"

"Why not, just not in exhaustive detail."

"We generate rubrics, vectors and variables in seventeen categories, establish standard deviations, determine reliability and validity quotients. . . I could go on if you like."

"Please don't."

"You disagree that thorough assessment is essential if the University is to achieve its full potential?"

Uwe sipped his coffee. "No good organization is perfect and no perfect organization is good," he said sententiously.

"Ah. That checks out."

"Pardon me?"

"In your undergraduate philosophy course, you rated Aristotle above Plato."

"I prefer *reading* Plato; who wouldn't? But in my opinion, Aristotle was right about so much only because Plato was so much more brilliantly wrong."

"That sounds just like something a popular docent would say, a real academic *bon mot*. Clever and memorable. In fact, you've said it five times, verbatim, in the last three semesters."

"Is there something wrong with that?"

"Not at all. Sincerity and spontaneity are of no quantitative interest."

"And yet they are of enormous qualitative significance."

"Then why do you repeat what might have been spontaneous the first time but not the next two?"

"You know nothing of the theater, do you?"

"Hardly anything. Do you mean you see a classroom as a stage?"

"I do, and for good reason. An actor has to repeat himself, but Hamlet must always ask 'To be or not to be' for the first time."

"I don't understand."

"No, I expect you don't."

"No call for condescension, Uwe, especially when it's you who's missing the point, not me. I don't think you fail to appreciate how important this project is to your Chancellor."

"And also to your gravy train?"

Mock laughed, more loudly this time and with more sincerity. "Not at all. Our company's services are in high demand. Business was up 37.4% in the last quarter alone."

"How much of the 37.4% was from universities?"

"97.3%."

"I see."

"Do you? Like your Chancellor, the real educational leaders have all grasped the superiority of data to sentimentality, of numbers to anecdotes, the imperative to base all judgments on metrics."

"It's true. The Chancellor's favorite word is *metrics*. He deploys it often, rather like a halberd. And yet, to my knowledge, he's never delivered a speech in anapestic hexameter."

"Very amusing in the faculty dining room, I'm sure. But your joke shows that poetry too is number."

Uwe sighed. "And yet numbers are so seldom poetry. In fact, they're more usually prices. I wonder, Herr Bock, what you Pythagoreans do for fun."

"Word problems and sudoku. Once, my department went to a karaoke bar and got drunk. The evening, I'll admit, was not an unqualified success. But it was fun all the same."

"Karaoke? What did you sing? I'm really curious."

"I finished off the evening with an old lullaby my grandmother used to sing to me."

"How sweet. What was it?"

"*Eins, Zwei, Polizei.*"

"Polizei? Am I under arrest, then?"

Mock smiled but not cordially. "You'll have your joke, of course. On the other hand, if you insist on not completing our questionnaire, I can't rule out that your position may be in some jeopardy. The Faculty of German Language and Literature currently employs fifteen docents, a number somewhat surplus to requirements by our reckoning. It could easily make do with fourteen—even thirteen."

Uwe calmly sipped his coffee. "Why don't you take a seat, Herr Mock? There's something I want to ask you."

Mock remained by the counter, as if bonded with Uwe's coffee-maker, and looked down on Uwe, mockingly. "I prefer to stand. What do you want to know?"

"Well, I suppose you'd say it's about your business model."

"Yes?"

"As I understand things, your firm's principal metric of faculty excellence is not how many articles and books we publish, but how often those publications are cited by other scholars in *their* publications."

Mock looked slightly impressed. "That is correct."

"Good. Now, let's suppose I write an article about Heinrich von Kleist's story *Michael Kohlhaas.*"

"Made from the conference paper you delivered a year ago last November?"

This time it was Uwe who smiled. "No, something entirely different. In this article I present a new interpretation of the story. I argue that it is a symbolic displacement of the author's mad plan to assassinate Napoleon Bonaparte whom he represents in the nasty and rapacious character of Wenzel von Tronka. Kohlhaas's ferocious attack on Castle Tronka, the three attempts to burn down Wittenberg—a stand-in for Paris—are all expressions of Kleist's urge toward violent and patriotic retaliation. It took Kleist years to find his way out of the story and, during this time, he shifted the role of his protagonist so that, in the conclusion of the story it's Kohlhaas who represents Napoleon as, in his megalomania, he declares himself the head of a 'provisional world government'. The beheading of Kohlhaas on the order of the Holy Roman Emperor is Kleist's scarcely veiled plea for all of Europe to unite against the French tyrant."

"Did Kleist really plan to kill Bonaparte?"

"Yes."

"I've heard of Kleist, of course, but I didn't know that."

"It's beside the point."

"Which is?"

"Let's say I succeed in getting this ridiculous article published, accepted perhaps by an editor with a sense of humor. Now, suppose every essay published about *Michael Kohlhaas* for the next decade includes a footnote that reads, more or less, 'For a truly bone-headed interpretation of Kleist's story see Uwe von Gerstenberg, "Kleist's Crypto-Politics: *Michael Kohlhaas* and the Assassination of Napoleon Bonaparte."'"

"And your question is?"

"Would Bildungsanalytik, GmbH, applying its rubrics, quotients, and metrics of assessment, report that I am an ornament of the University?"

"That's absurd."

"Agreed. But is it true, Herr Mock?"

Mock's smile had a touch of menace in it. "You're a stiff-necked one, Uwe. Why are you so stubborn, so hostile? After all, it's only a questionnaire?"

"One that would require no more than eleven minutes to complete. I know. But you're quite right, Herr Mock; I am hostile to your work."

"Then you don't understand it."

"I understand very well why the Chancellor likes assessment or at least sees it as part of his job. I understand why he wants your metrics, numbers, graphs, and charts. It's because they can all be read quickly; it's because they amalgamate *numbers* of articles and people into *amounts* of people and articles. It's because he believes that quantities reveal qualities, which I do not. In the end, the purpose of it all is simply to judge our lectures without listening to them and our publications without reading them."

"But to do what you're suggesting would be not just logistically unfeasible but also so subjective as to be of no statistical or administrative value."

"Yes, it's absurd, just as you say. Prohibitively inefficient and unreliable. Contrary to the needs of administration."

"Then you *do* grant the premise of our work?"

"No, Herr Mock. Precisely the opposite. Perhaps I can explain by telling you a story."

"I'd prefer a completed questionnaire, Uwe."

"Nevertheless. Here, do sit down."

Mock unconsciously stroked his thighs, as if to reassure himself that the crease in his trousers was as sharp as ever. Then he sat.

"Good. Three years ago, the University's newly appointed head of Pedagogical Information Technology was making the rounds and invited himself to a meeting of our faculty. He was a man of no more than twenty-five, not nearly so well dressed as yourself, nor as cordial. I had the impression that he did share your confidence, though."

"Confidence?"

"The intoxicating feeling that comes when you're certain you possess the kind of knowledge that's power and that others don't."

"You think that's what confidence is?"

Uwe smiled sweetly. "It's a politer word than arrogance. Anyway, our youthful IT chief took the podium from the dean and began by saying that he had actually spent the entire afternoon in our building, standing outside doors, peeking into classrooms and eavesdropping on what was going on in them. For a nano-second I thought what he said next was the highest compliment he could possibly pay us. He said, 'I didn't see or hear anything that Socrates wouldn't have understood.' In the next nano-second, I realized that what I'd taken for praise was meant as the opposite. And a nano-second after *that*, I concluded that he and I would never see things the same way. And that, you could say, is why I declined to complete your questionnaire."

Jürgen Mock rose, again checked the crease in his trousers, pulled down the sleeves of his suit jacket, not neglecting first to make a note of the time on his wristwatch, then deposited his coffee mug in the sink. Looking down on Uwe with a rueful smile, he shook his head twice and walked to the door without another word.

3. *Un Morceau de Justice - Septuor Chinoise pour Cordes en do-majeur avec un Début Triste et Fin Gratifiante*

The Empire was in the hands of a cruel ruler, obsessed with completing the Grand Canal, restoring the Great Wall, and conquering Goguryeo. The number of lives sacrificed to the first two enterprises is beyond counting; but, for his third and last campaign against Goguryeo, the lives were counted to a man and recorded. 305,000 marched across the frontier; 2700 returned.

Song Yu made his farewells to the other survivors three days after they dragged themselves across the border at Liadong, defeated, terrified, starved. They looked angrily and greedily at the heaps of supplies the army was supposed to have reached them a month before. The troops at the depot regarded the filthy and thin veterans. The officers refused to believe their story, accused them of desertion, and put them under guard. They were only released the next morning when Captain Suh staggered in with three horsemen and their two pitiable mounts. When Suh, his stern face running with tears, confirmed their account of the rout, Song and the others were released. At once they fell on the supplies and gorged themselves. Then they curled up among the bales and boxes and slept like corpses until the next day after the sun was well up.

Song had heard that in his youth Yang Guang showed himself a talented poet and a deplorable human being. He had proved a ruinous emperor, an unfit successor to the esteemed Wendi, who unified the Empire, restored the government, and built many temples. Song began to believe the rumor that Yang had assassinated his father. He also decided to leave the army, simply to walk away. In the East, there was no army left anyway. His plan was to walk to his village in Jingzhou. It had been three years since he was conscripted at the age of seventeen, and he longed to see his parents, his siblings, all his cousins, aunts, and uncles.

It was high summer and the fields looked green, abundant. But the villages he passed through felt depopulated and sullen. There were only old men, women, and children who looked indifferent or lost. He knew that those men who had not been sent north to work on the Wall or south to dig the Canal would have marched east into Goguryeo. He did not want to tell people about the campaign; yet none of the women who gave him a place to sleep or shared their soup and rice asked.

Perhaps, he thought, they're already resigned. Few returned from the Wall or the Canal either. He knew well the fatalism of peasants.

Song arrived at the large village of Boling late in the day and during a rainstorm. As he passed a hut, drenched to the skin, an old man appeared in the doorway and with a big smile motioned for him to come in out of the rain. It had been a long time since Song had seen anyone smile like that.

Lyu Yingzhe introduced himself and said that he lived with his son's wife and his two grandchildren. "We grow three kinds of radishes, bok choy, and rice, some wheat." He pointed to a dilapidated shed. "We keep pigs as well, the best in the whole district. The landlord will buy only from us." Peasants can be proud as well as resigned.

Song gave his name and explained where he was headed.

"Jingzhou! That must be a long way off."

"Long enough."

"You're all wet. Come in. We'll warm you up and you can spend the night here."

The old man called for his daughter-in-law, who bowed to Song. He asked her to fetch some of her husband's old clothes and build up the fire. Song changed behind an old screen, and she laid his things out to dry. It was strange wearing another man's clothes, being with his wife and father.

The two little children, a boy and a girl, had run to their bed as soon as Song entered the hut and pulled the quilt over their heads. Now they peered out at him curiously. He gave them a wink.

Lyu's daughter-in-law knew the way to make simple food delicious. She treated the guest with courtesy. To her father-in-law she was respectful without being servile and, with the children, at once firm and loving.

When the sun was down, Lyu insisted the guest share his pallet and worn blanket. Once he was sure the others were asleep, Lyu elbowed Song and whispered, "Come with me."

They went out into the summer night. The moon was almost at the full and peeked out, like the children, from between thin clouds.

Song had thought Lyu wanted to check the pigs, but his purpose was to ask about Goguryeo.

"There are terrible rumors," he said.

"Why do you think I'd know?"

Lyu frowned. "You're about my son's age. You've still got all your limbs and you're traveling west which means you aren't coming from either the Wall or the Canal. So, you must have been in the Emperor's army."

"I can't deny it."

"Then tell me what happened, no matter how bad. I can bear it. I'm a veteran myself. I fought the Turks."

A burden shared is half as heavy, says the proverb; and it really was a relief to Song to speak of what he'd been through. Song told how the crafty Mundeok had sent small detachments to harass them, hitting and running, all the while leading them deeper into the country, always in the direction of their goal, the capital. He told how the supplies never arrived, that some died of hunger, but the generals commanded them to press on, promising everything they needed would be arriving the next day. At last, he told what had happened at Salsu River, how Mundeok had had it dammed, cutting the flow so that it was only a shallow stream between high banks when the army began to ford it.

"The officers ordered us to cross in a broad front rather than in columns, to be ready in case of an ambush on the other side which was heavily wooded. When we were in the middle of the riverbed, Mundeok had the dam broken open and the river came down on us like a divine judgment. Thousands drowned. Then their cavalry came out of the woods, screaming like barbarians. The few of us who survived ran in a panic back the way we'd come. Many died of exhaustion or starvation. We'd eaten up all the crops we could find during our march and making a wasteland for ourselves. If your son was with us, I fear he won't be coming home. I'm sorry."

The old soldier nodded once, stiffly, as if what he'd just heard wasn't news but a confirmation.

In the morning, Song thanked everyone and asked if he could perhaps help with some of the heavier chores before going on his way.

"The roof could use some repairs," said Lyu.

"The woodpile," said the daughter-in-law shyly.

Song spent the morning fixing thatch and chopping wood. "You'll spend another night," said the daughter-in-law when she brought him tea and bing cakes.

After replenishing the woodpile, he taught the children to play Catch the Dragon's Tail. Their screams and laughter were better than any tune from a bamboo flute.

Over supper, Song asked about conditions in the village and, knowing how things worked, whether their landlord was a good or a bad man.

Lyu and his daughter exchanged a glance.

"After the children go to sleep," said the old man.

"Father?" said the woman anxiously.

"It's all right. He'll be leaving."

The night was even more pleasant than the last. Lyu and Song took stools outside and Song heard the story of the landlord, Chiang

Hongxu, his second wife, Pingyang, and his two daughters, Shih and Ching-ling.

As the wealthiest man in the district, the one from whom most of the peasants rented their land, Chiang and his household were not spoken in public but closely watched.

"Everybody knows what's been going on in that family, but nobody says anything. They're afraid of Chiang's temper, though he's not really a bad man."

"Not bad?"

"Only deceived," said Lyu.

"How?"

Lyu hesitated only briefly, then went on at length.

"Nobody liked the first wife. She was vain, greedy, and cold. When that fever took her, Chiang was left with the two girls. They already resembled their mother, but he doted on them. So, he needed a wife. Pingyang is the youngest child of Huang Hui-liang who was deep in debt to Chiang and so it was arranged. Pingyang is only a few years older than her stepdaughters who were not pleased. They felt superior to Pingyang and let her know it. She is humble and modest, soft-spoken and also very pretty. Chiang grew fond of her. He even chided the girls for showing no gratitude for all she did for them. This only made them more hostile to Pingyang whom they saw as their slave. So, they got their friends to start a rumor that she'd been seen flirting with Chu, the young bailiff. They arranged that the rumor would get back to their father. He confronted Pingyang. What could the girl do but deny it? Chiang was furious. It seems he thought of sending her back to her father, but he still needed her to run the household and wait on his daughters. So, he dismissed his servant Bao-zhai and handed all his work over to his wife. Not satisfied, the girls constantly made up complaints to tell their father about their poor stepmother. The more they slandered and tyrannized over her, the more they played up to

Chiang." Lyu shook his head. "The man must be blind. He can't see the truth. He appeases the girls by buying them things. Some say he beats Pingyang, and everybody's seen how rough he is with her. The girl bears everything without complaint."

Song knew that injustices were beyond counting and understood the imperfection of the world. He saw how the extravagant ambition of an inhumane ruler sowed misery across the empire. He knew Lyu would never again see his son, that widows wail and children forget dead fathers. About such things, he could do nothing. Yet Lyu's story had moved him; and, as if it might make up a little for all he couldn't do, Song resolved to achieve a small measure of justice in this village, one not so different from his own in Jingzhou.

It took Song two days to come up with half a plan. He would require Lyu's help but not in any way that would risk the displeasure of his landlord. He asked two things of the old man: first, to point out Pingyang; second, to let her husband know that a stranger had arrived with news from Goguryeo. He wanted to get some sense of the woman, and he guessed that Chiang, as the richest man in the district, would think he also ought to be the best informed. Beyond seeing Pingyang and meeting with Chiang he had not thought.

Lyu agreed. "Pingyang fetches water from the well at least twice a day. As for Chiang, I can ask to see him about delivering the pig and drop a word about you."

The next morning, the two men went to the village center. Pingyang soon arrived with her buckets and yoke. Song saw that she was pretty but worn down and noted how shabbily she was dressed. When she leaned over the well, he observed that she wore a string necklace with a pendant of green jade. The jade seemed out of place, and he asked Lyu if he knew anything about it.

"That piece of carved jade is the one thing she has from her father. It's her one personal possession. She's never seen without it."

Then Lyu pointed to two adolescent girls who had strolled into the square. They were dressed in colorful silk robes and had elaborate hair arrangements. They went at once to the merchant who sold luxury goods. They looked at him haughtily and he bowed.

"Shih and Ching-ling," Lyu whispered.

That night Song recalled a story he'd been told by his grandmother about Emperor Wendi's consort, his beloved Dugu. The Emperor loved Dugu faithfully. He prized her intelligence and also her frugality. When he came down with diarrhea, the court physicians recommended a medicine that required a quantity of black pepper, a spice more expensive than gold. The court ladies prized it as a cosmetic. When Wendi asked Dugu for some her stock, she replied that she had none because it was too costly.

Song had calculated correctly. Shortly after Lyu went to see Chiang about the pig, a boy arrived at the hut inviting the stranger who had been in Goguryeo to dinner.

Chiang's villa was the finest house in the village, with two red-painted pillars in front and a tiled roof. The landlord greeted Song with courtesy but distantly.

During the meal, the girls flirted with Song openly but not seriously, as if practicing their skills by competing for his admiration. After all, they rarely saw a young man. The meal was served by Pingyang. Song thanked her for each dish. Chiang and his daughters entirely ignored her.

Song delivered a sanitized version of the catastrophe then suggested that, if Chiang desired more details, he should excuse the girls to avoid offending their sensibilities. This Chiang did. He wanted to know everything.,

After hearing Song's account of the army's suffering and the catastrophe at the river, Chiang sighed.

"It's terrible. It could even mean the end for the Sui. But what's to be done?"

He rose, went to a cabinet, and drew out two wooden cups and a jug of yellow wine.

"At least we can drink." And they did.

Once Chiang had become a little tipsy, Song asked about the woman who had served them. "Is she your only servant?"

"That's my wife, my second wife."

When Song expressed surprise that she had not dined with them, Chiang launched into the story Song had heard from Lyu about Chu the bailiff and the catalogue of the daughters' false complaints.

"Are you sure your wife doesn't love or respect you?"

"She is a slut who comes from nothing. She fears me, no more."

"And your daughters?"

"What? My precious nestlings? They love me dearly. They tell me so three times a day!"

Song was quiet for a while, drinking. "What if you tested them?"

"What?"

"I noticed that your daughters, though they hardly need them, use cosmetics."

"What of it?"

Song laid out his idea. "First check to see if your daughters have a supply of black pepper. If they do, pretend to have a stomach ailment and tell them your doctor has prescribed a medicine requiring ground pepper and ask to give you all they have."

Chiang objected that such a test was unnecessary, but Song persisted until he had made his host angry enough to agree.

The girls did have a supply of black pepper but when their father asked them for it, they claimed to have none. Pingyang, overhearing the conversation, went to the market where she sought out the luxury merchant and exchanged her jade pendant for his half his supply of pepper.

After weeding the field and feeding the pigs, Song thanked Lyu and his family profusely for their unforgettable hospitality then went on his way. He left too early to witness all the changes in the Chiang household. Shih was married off to an elderly widower and Ching-ling given the choice of becoming a Buddhist nun or taking on all the tasks formerly assigned to her stepmother, whose pendant Chiang redeemed and whom he now treated with a loving tenderness fortified by remorse.

Song's long journey ended with a happy reunion and many tears. When Yangdi, from whom Heaven had withdrawn its mandate, was strangled by his generals and the new Tang dynasty began, Song was appointed to the position of district magistrate, a job he carried out with both justice and compassion.

Petite Suite Ordinateur

1. *Algorithme Tordu – Trio Menaçante en si-mineur pour Violoncelle et Clarinette Juive avec Lecteur Électronique Obligato*

David was away on business again. Was it Toledo this time or Cleveland? It would be awkward to ask. For the last two months, he phoned every night he was away and always began, "How are you?" But Eleanor soon felt his concern was less about her than the fetus, which at first David called the schmitzik and then just Schmitzik. He thought it cute, Yiddish, affectionate, and loving. Eleanor didn't like it, but she played along as in "Schmitzik kicked like a Rockette all afternoon."

Eleanor was twenty-six, in her eighth month, on maternity leave from a job she liked and missed. She was bored and discontent. David, a technophile fond of digital fixes, bought her a Kindle and she'd been reading a lot of new fiction on it. But she had grown tired of contemporary novels, the funny ones no less than the serious. Now she wanted something that wasn't new at all, something by an uncontemporary female with an old-fashioned vocabulary, a Brontë sister or George Eliot. Then she thought of *Frankenstein* which had been assigned in a freshman literature course. At the time, she'd thought the instructor made too little of the book, and especially of the teenager who wrote it. She downloaded the book and read it over two days.

Eleanor looked up Mary Shelley on the computer and learned a lot. Mary was pregnant more or less continuously from the time she met her already-married, Oxford-expelled poet-husband until he drowned. When she began on the book, she'd already lost a baby. Her gifted feminist mother had died giving her birth. While she was working on the novel, her favorite half-sister committed suicide and so did Shelley's first wife. She had all these deaths on her record, and she was only eighteen. "*I not in deed but in effect was the true murderer*," says Victor. Maybe that indirect guilt was the emotional core of Mary's inspired nightmare. Even as she was wielding her pen, Mary was nursing her second baby, little William. This gave Eleanor a jolt. The Monster's first victim is a little boy she could have named Fritz or Heinrich but called William, not even Wilhelm. Sex equals death? Was that what was on Mary's subconscious mind? Elizabeth Lavenza is strangled on her wedding night, on the marriage bed. The fair-haired orphan, is Mary, but Mary corrected, Mary in the family but also not as the author was when her father remarried, but Mary made proper, ordinary, and submissive, somebody else's ego-ideal—and even the perfect Elizabeth accidentally kills her adopted mother. Victor and Elizabeth grew up together. Frau Frankenstein's dying wish is that they marry. Well, thought Eleanor, Victor claims to love Liz but he doesn't visit once or even write a letter to her after he gets away to Ingolstadt. On the evidence, what Victor really loves—at least until he finishes the project—is digging up gigantic German corpses and sewing them together; he is the scientist who, mad or sane, adores his work *über alles*—and perhaps the teenage author did too. Eleanor recalled something a football coach said about a big game that ended in a tie—"It's like kissing your sister." So, Victor is Mary too. Don't they both make monsters? Eleanor continued riffing on the idea that all the main characters are Mary, pregnant like herself. Aren't babies little monsters—noisy, needy, barbaric? Of course, Mary is the Monster too—motherless, abandoned, big, clumsy, a clever outsider, seething with resentment, a murderer looking for love. Victor's creature is no Godzilla, no mindless mass murderer. He only wipes out one family, perhaps stand-ins for Mary's hyphenated relatives whom she claimed to love so much.

Mary killed her mother, baby, sister, her husband's wife, and was perpetually enceinte. Pregnancy thickens your ankles, swells your breasts, widens your hips, turns your thighs heavy and your face puffy. You stagger around with big, wide steps—just like Boris Karloff. That's the way Eleanor walked now. One night when David was away, she stripped down and checked herself out in the full-length mirror. She wanted to see what David saw. The sweet-faced sylph he had married had gone. What she saw was a monster.

People phoned you on their schedule, including David. Eleanor preferred emails you could deal with in your own sweet time. One morning when she booted up there was an email from Amazon. Nothing surprising in that, but it wasn't about anything she'd bought—or bought yet. It said " WE FOUND SOMETHING YOU MIGHT LIKE" next to a book cover. She figured she must have downloaded whatever number of e-books qualified you for a marketing algorithm and the illusion that Amazon was looking out for you. But when she examined the book cover, it chilled her. The name of the author of *The Greatest Punishment* rang a bell. Amado Pereira. It took only a second to summon up the memory of the skinny, unathletic, olive-skinned, dark-haired, bookish, shy loner with the outlandish name who had an irrepressible crush on her ten years before. But how could Amazon know that? She clicked on the book cover. The novel's Amazon number was 8,577,406. Well, it might have sold well when it came out two years earlier. She clicked to the back cover to see if there was an author photo. There was, in stark black-and-white. Still olive-skinned and looking almost angry in his earnestness, it was the boy, but the boy filled out and with a short beard that suited him. Amado Pereira, the author, was handsome. She could imagine Victor Frankenstein looking just as intense.

The Author Note said he taught at a college she'd never heard of in Texas and that this was his first novel. And that was it—nothing about a wife or children or cats.

How many times had they spoken? Only once, twice? She hadn't been very nice to him.

They didn't have any classes together but he'd staked out her locker for months, like a wolf hovering near a flock, focused on one appetizing ewe. Eleanor remembered how everybody was always checking each other out in that hormonal hothouse. She was no different, sensitized to register male interest the way girls do, and Amado's was confirmed by Jillian and Sasha, the way high-school girls love to do. They teased her; they thought it was funny. "You going to put him out of his misery?" "Bet he asks you to the prom!"

He hadn't done that, but he did take one shot. She'd been alone in the cafeteria for once and he seized the moment to sit down across from her. He'd been so pathetically awkward, so formal. He almost held out his hand then didn't. "Pardon me. I know you're Eleanor Minghetti. I'm Amado, Amado Pereira." Had he been watching Bond movies?

"Pereira. Is that, what? Portuguese?"

"Sephardic," he'd said, in a way that had seemed to her a little defensive or peeved.

"It's a nice name. Amado. Unusual."

He'd made a face and she thought he'd have been happier had his parents gone for Chuck or Bruce.

He blurted it out, all hope and audacity. "Would you like to go skating with me Friday night? The rink's still open."

Eleanor had thanked him and said she was busy Friday—Saturday too. His face collapsed; he polished off his sandwich in two bites and fled.

He'd never tried again. After that, the locker-hovering let up, though it didn't stop completely. Or maybe it hadn't let up at all and she just stopped noticing.

Pereira had two books on Amazon. The other was a collection of stories titled *To See What I Have Seen, See What I See* published by an obscure press. Its Amazon number was astronomical.

Eleanor downloaded the novel. The epigraph explained the title.

To burn with desire and keep quiet about it is the greatest punishment we can bring on ourselves.

-Federico Garcia Lorca

The book was, like nearly all first novels, autobiographical. It started off as a standard bildungsroman: intelligent, sensitive kid from an immigrant family who switches codes between home and school and feels out of place in both, lots of interior monologuing, lengthy reflections on literary and musical enthusiasms, self-mockery and grandiose ambitions. But then it took a turn. In his last year of high school, the protagonist, Aaron Pandev, becomes infatuated with a girl. Her name is Ellen. She's beautiful, popular—leagues out of his league. Several chapters are devoted to his careful observations of how Ellen dresses, her friends, her moods, her many virtues, few flaws, and various parts of her body. It took him three chapters to work his way up to speaking to her. For Aaron, the prospect is like the one at the edge of a cliff, fascinating, even irresistible, yet terrifying. It finally happens. He sees her one afternoon outside the town library, steels himself, and leaps.

When he asks her out to see a Bergman film, she gives a sort of quarter-laugh, an involuntary plosive, then declines with laudable courtesy. But she'd laughed first, the worst kind of laugh, an involuntary one.

Crushed, Aaron doesn't stop thinking about Ellen. On the contrary—he thinks of her more and more, too much. The obsession takes over his life. He tries to slough it off, but can't escape, not into books or music or Stoic resignation or even college. His monologues become ever more deranged. He composes poems made terrible by their sincerity.

The novel winds up with Aaron taking a bus from his rural college into the city, buying a pistol, and trying to decide whether to shoot himself or Ellen or first Ellen and then himself.

Eleanor wrapped her Kindle in a dish towel and buried it at the bottom of her sweater drawer.

Schmitzik kicked all the way through dinner.

At eight o'clock on the dot, David called from either Toledo or Cleveland.

2. *Romance Taquine, Oratorio Académique, Brève et Indécis, pour Mezzo-Soprano Agacée, Ténor Aggravé, et Choeur Exaspérant, en la-majeur*

Notwithstanding his status as an eminent expert on econometrics, Professor Stephen Chen was an inveterate tease. He looked like a Buddhist monk and often spoke like a Borscht-Belt comedian. "Teasing," Chen once explained after entertaining somebody's obstreperous seven-year-old with it for half an hour, "is a way of keeping the world at bay by appearing to invite yourself in. Children who understand teasing enjoy it. The ones who don't resent it. It's no different with grownups." It was from this congenial senior colleague that Harold Altenberg first learned about his affair with Janet D'Alessandro.

Professor Chen had just put an end to a department meeting by requesting a straw vote. "Everybody who thinks the matter of grade inflation was more than adequately addressed at the *last* two of these meetings, please raise your hand."

Robin Maguire was department chairman only because it was his turn in the rotation. He set the agenda. This was his first semester in the chair and, as he was not, like Chen, a full professor but a newly tenured associate, he approached the job earnestly. He looked around the conference table, defeated. When he raised his hand, everybody laughed and made for the door.

It was on their way out that Stephen Chen nudged Harold and whispered, "Your divorce is behind you, Harold. Time to move on. So, good. I hope it's true about, well, you know."

"What?"

"Oh, that's right. I forgot you don't do social media. Sorry. But everybody else does."

"What are you talking about?"

"Hashtag D'Alessandro and Altenberg," said Chen with a wink and sauntered down the hallway, chortling. Harold was flummoxed, a little horrified but also just a little tickled.

Janet D'Alessandro, Assistant Professor of Chemistry, pretended not to notice the suppressed giggles and furtive looks of her female students and tried not to guess at the remarks traded by the males. She was in the fourth year of her probationary period; a tenure decision was only two years off—if she was even kept on, let alone allowed to apply.

Her Organic Chemistry class was mobbed, perhaps more because it was a requirement for so many students than because of her pedagogical gifts, though her evaluations were good. She had five articles in good journals and a respectable list of symposia and conference presentations.

By being hit on all through high school, college, grad school, and even during her post-doc year, she had learned to be professional, to insist on being addressed by her surname, preferably preceded by "Doctor". She had learned that the combination of chilly seriousness and unconcealable good looks could be attractive to many men and some women. She always wore either a lab coat or a blazer, never anything tight, bright, or short. When she became aware about the rumor by reading the gleeful online gossip, what she felt first was indignation, a frustrated ambition, the disappointment of parents. She didn't know anything about Harold Altenberg until she looked him up. A labor economist.

What could she do? This could be dangerous.

Janet made pre-emptive appointment with the Dean, a thin man with a carefully trimmed beard who had wearied of medieval history, took to administration like a bully to a schoolyard, and always looked terribly busy. He was dismissive.

"Ignore it and it'll peter out." He ventured a smile that looked vaguely salacious. "Best not to, uh, protest too much."

It didn't peter out, and the lawyer she was dating, a plausible prospect, didn't think it was a prank. She tried laughing it off, explaining about weeder courses, then denials that sounded desperate even to her. In the end, the attorney did think she protested too much, mumbled something about smoke and fire, and stopped calling.

Harold Altenberg didn't call either, but he did send an email.

Dear Professor D'Alessandro,

Well, it appears we're in a fix. #D'Alessandro and Altenberg.

I've no idea who started this business or why and I'm as miffed about it as I imagine you are. Funny looks, people who stop talking when they see you, unfunny teasing from colleagues. Same with you? It's all infuriating.

Maybe we should talk.

While Janet wasn't thrilled to hear from Harold Altenberg, she didn't dislike the tone of his email. She knew she had to write some sort of reply but hesitated about the suggestion to meet. What if they were seen together?

Professor Altenberg,

Thank you for your email. I don't know what we can do. I'm willing to meet to talk about it but, for obvious reasons, not on campus.

They agreed on a Friday night dinner at a small but pretentious French restaurant too expensive for students and one town away from the University.

Harold had on a Harris tweed jacket and a light blue tie that almost matched his eyes. Janet wore a severely tailored navy-blue suit, appropriate for jury duty or a funeral. He ordered the boeuf bourguignon. She said she'd like to try the salmon en papillote. The waiter congratulated her and inquired about the wine. Harold and Janet looked at each other and shrugged simultaneously. That made them smile.

The waiter hastened to help. "May I suggest a light pinot noir? It's one of the few wines that goes with both beef and fish."

Harold looked at Janet who nodded. "Okay," he said.

Harold told Janet how he'd learned of the mess from Professor Chen. That prompted her to share the story of her unsatisfactory visit with the Dean.

Deploring their hashtag to one another was a relief to both, but neither knew what to do about it.

The conversation shifted to academic politics, how they chose their disciplines, Janet's tenure prospects, Harold's research on productivity rises in relation to income distribution. They had a lot to say to each other.

A nod to the inquiring waiter resulted a second bottle of pinot noir.

"It's funny, in a way," Harold said because of the wine.

"Funny how?"

He blushed, despite the wine. "Because—how can I put it?—because I noticed you."

"Noticed?"

"Um, well, I saw you at a faculty meeting. You spoke about the new general education proposal. Not enough science. Remember?"

"I remember."

He looked down at the remains of his chocolate mousse.

"I even asked somebody about you, who you were."

She pouted. "Ah ha. Maybe *that's* how it got started."

"I apologize." Then, remembering what a student had said after giving a wrong answer in class, he added, "My bad."

Janet was surprised that she didn't feel angry at all. "Yes," she said. "You're bad."

At their second dinner a week later—Italian this time—the topics were their parents, siblings, why they hated high school, their job searches and interviews, anecdotes about good students and bad ones, a little gossip about colleagues.

At the third dinner—at a steakhouse—Harold talked in some detail about his divorce, and she told him about the lawyer's abrupt decamping.

Not long after Janet and Harold began meeting regularly for lunch on campus, the social media chatter, puerile tittering, and collegial teasing dwindled to nothing.

3. *Cycles Cycliques, Quatuor Errant et Parcheminesque, pour Liuqin, Groupe Chinoise, Diplomate, et Mur, en sol-majeur*

Except for the rare evening when he went out, Joshua Rinehart pedaled ten miles between five and five-forty p.m. in front of the TV.

On weekends, he biked to whatever sport was on, even golf. There was no one to stop him, to insist he listen to her, to complain about the noise. Divorce was liberating and changed him in several ways; his cycling routine was only one. Another was a willingness to spend money on himself.

Joshua bought a flat-screen TV and set it up on in front of his chain-driven Huffy, a hand-me-down from his ex-brother-in-law. He was surprised by how cheap the TV was and how good. The brand said *Belmont*, but the tag said *Made in China*. Now, he watched the evening news three times: Deutsche Welle at five, then the BBC, and, while he cooked his dinner and ate it, PBS. He liked contrasting what the Germans thought should lead off the news to what the Brits and the Americans thought most urgent. Best of all were the local stories: Neo-Nazis marching through Schönberg, an eccentric in Salisbury with the world's largest collection of naturist magazines, a family in Arkansas with eight children, all chess prodigies.

The venerable Huffy needed frequent tinkering. Its chain was forever coming off the sprockets, and the thing was so loud that, even with the Belmont's volume at 100, Joshua had to strain to pick up the British disdain and Teutonic Schadenfreude in the news readers' voices. One evening, in the middle of a story about why the Bundesliga didn't deserve to be called the Farmers' League, the chain broke, and the steel wheel spun from its hub and crashed to the floor. *Huffy wurde kaputt*.

Joshua stared at the ruin with shock then relief. He realized he had long disliked the Huffy and could now replace it.

After dinner he went straight to Amazon.com. Even the cheapest models looked better than the Huffy—no big wheel or chain, collapsible. They came with battery-powered gizmos and solemn promises of quiet operation and easy assembly, all for under two hundred bucks. The Chinese TV was good; why wouldn't ChinaExport's Yundong Model-5 be as well? He placed his order. Delivery was predicted within twelve days.

Three weeks later Joshua arrived home from work to find a large oblong crate deposited at his door. The thing weighed a ton; the UPS driver must have used a dolly. The label indicated it had shipped from ChinaExport's warehouse in El Monte, California, but the shape and weight didn't suggest there was a bike inside, even an unassembled one made of lead. Grunting, sweating, and hoping not to rupture himself, Joshua wrangled the thing over the threshold. He fetched a hammer and screwdriver and set about opening the thing which was almost as hard as getting it inside. The crate contained a set of weights, the circular, pumping-iron kind, a whole cycle of them from fifteen to fifty kilograms.

ChinaExport's customer service number's service was a looped program of easy-listening music interrupted every three minutes by a recorded assurance of how much the company cherished his call. After five assurances, he hung up and sent off an email with his order number explaining the error and requesting advice. He had a detailed reply the next day. This conveyed humble apologies, chagrin at the mistake, heartfelt regret and sincere embarrassment followed by a pre-paid UPS label to print out for returning the weights. He did his best to reconstruct the crate and arranged a time for it to be picked up. "Bring a dolly or send a weightlifter," he warned UPS. Five weeks later he received a second delivery from El Monte, a cube-shaped corrugated cardboard box this time. It too was weighty and didn't have a cycle inside, just a lot of books in Mandarin. His best guess was that it was a set of encyclopedias. Well, he said to himself, at least *encyclopedia* had *cycle* in it. Though exasperated with ChinaExport, he was amused.

This time Joshua didn't bother phoning; he went straight to email. Two days later came a reply with an apology that was just as lengthy as the first and another pre-paid label. He summoned UPS.

The third delivery came three weeks later, was a stout wooden crate, smaller and lighter than the first one, heavily reinforced with metal strips, so that it looked like an old-fashioned strongbox. Inside, surrounded in layers of bubble-wrap over strips of bamboo atop soft cloth, Joshua found four scrolls. He could see at one that they were very old and fragile. He cleared the dining room table, fetched sixteen books, removed each scroll with care, laid them out and placed a book in each corner. The scrolls were of uniform size, about twelve by twenty-four inches, and what was painted on them was a series of exquisite marvels. They all depicted a landscape of mountains and boulders with a waterfall, lake, and a forested bank in each of the four seasons. *Another cycle*, thought Joshua who had already fallen in love with the pictures.

That same evening, he got a phone call from a number he didn't recognize and so ignored. Minutes later came an email with a red "high priority" exclamation point. It was from ChinaExport's Vice President for the Americas, who signed himself unpretentiously Bill Chung. Albeit in a controlled way, Bill beside himself. He began with the formulaic thousand apologies for all the mix-ups, all his company's inexcusable mistakes. "Be assured, heads will roll," he wrote, and Joshua briefly wondered if that might be literally true. The weights and the encyclopedias were bad enough, Bill confessed, but this latest glitch "took the cake". The four scrolls were not intended for him but, as a fraternal people-to-people gesture from the city of Shanghai, for temporary exhibition at the Joslyn Art Museum in Omaha, Nebraska. ChinaExport had been contracted by the Chinese government to handle the shipping. "We will be grateful for your help in seeing that the scrolls reach their intended destination. You will receive a phone call tomorrow from a DHL representative. You don't have to do a thing but open your door, Mr. Rinehart. DHL will see to the repacking and shipping of the scrolls. Again, we humbly apologize, beg your forgiveness, and thank you for your understanding. ChinaExport will be sending you a check for $500 and, of course, the cycle you ordered. Your payment for that item will be fully refunded with our enduring gratitude."

Joshua no longer needed the cycle, having long before bought a good used model off Ebay for $120. He had no intention of letting DHL into his house unless they were accompanied by a SWAT team with a warrant. He wrote back to Bill succinctly: "Please cancel my order for the Yundong Model 5. As for the $500, I suggest you send it to Omaha as compensation for the inconvenience."

Joshua was naturally eager to learn what he could about the paintings. He took a jpg of "Spring" and dropped it on Google Images. There it was—dozens of images. He clicked on the one from the Shanghai Museum and learned that the artist was Ko Qing-zhao described as one of the earliest masters of Shan Shui painting. Ko flourished during the latter part of the Sui Dynasty which, Joshua discovered, ended in 618 C.E. The paintings were, in the language of museum curators, priceless.

As he admired Ko's work, a phrase he hadn't used since fourth grade popped into Joshua's head, "Finders keepers."

He phoned his freshman roommate, Joe Bayuk, who was now practicing law in Chicago, told him the whole story, and asked how the law stood in such a case.

"I think you should return the pictures. I mean, *obviously*."

"Sure, but what does the law say."

Joe sighed. "Okay. I'll have an intern do the research. Look for an email in a day or two."

Joe's email arrived the next morning. It said the law recognized a distinction between *unsolicited goods*, those wrongly addressed, and a *mistaken delivery*, one addressed to somebody else and wrongly delivered. But the matter is ambiguous.

"As I understand things, the paintings are an 'unsolicited good' and, if you can persuade a judge to entertain that possibility, you can at least make an argument to keep them. Technically, if you didn't order something, you've no obligation either to return or pay for it. But the matter is complicated by your prior dealings with ChinaExport, their offer to arrange and pay for re-shipping and to compensate you. On top of that, of course, what you're proposing is to appropriate a Chinese national treasure."

Joshua called his friend. "Thanks for your advice, Joe" he said, "and thanks to that intern. I've only got one question. Can I be charged with a crime?"

"Well, not that I can see, but really, who knows? What you're doing is provocative, to put it mildly. Risky. I think if you try to hold on to those pictures you can pretty much count on your life being turned upside down."

Later in the day, Joshua got a call from DHL who wanted to arrange a time for the pick-up.

"Don't bother," he said and hung up.

The following day he received a certified letter delivered by courier. It was from the Chinese embassy and signed by the ambassador himself.

"We urge you to return the four items, as requested by our agent, ChinaExport, and to do so at once. The scrolls of Master Ko Qing-zhao are the property of the People's Republic of China. If you do not do as requested at once, we will be compelled to take legal action."

Joshua tossed the letter away.

That Sunday a well-groomed man in a good suit and bow tie showed up at his door. He identified himself as an official representative of the government and presented his card: Chester Arthur Whitmarsh, Office of Global Intergovernmental Affairs, State Department of the United States of America.

Joshua offered him coffee or tea.

Whitmarsh ignored this and asked to see the scrolls. Joshua directed him to the dining room table.

Whitmarsh didn't try to conceal his delight. On the contrary, he let out an unofficial gasp of appreciation. "My God!"

"They are really something, aren't they? I'm planning to have them framed," said Joshua. "What do you think—brown, black, red, or gold?"

Whitmarsh was horrified. He stressed the seriousness of the matter, said that it was a matter of national security and made clear that it was in Joshua's interest to cooperate promptly—pausing for the unspoken "or else". Aloud, he said more affably, "You'll have the gratitude of your government for doing so."

"I see," said Joshua, "big stick, tiny carrot. Look, I'm sorry, Mr. Whitmarsh—Chester—but I really prefer to keep the, um, unsolicited goods. I promise to have them insured though, for as much as I can afford. Now, if you'll be so kind as to leave, I want to get on my cycle. It's nearly time for the kickoff. Patriots versus Chiefs."

Petite Suite Onirique

1. Sors de Mes Rêves, S'il Te Plait - *Duo à sens unique en sol majeur pour violoncelle, lent avec un désespoir croissant.*

"This is just what I mean," he said. "Why are you here anyway? There's no reason for it."

Flat silence is different from not receiving a reply. The latter might mean somebody's at a loss or thinking up a plausible lie. They could be dumbfounded, nonplused, hard of hearing, but there is a likelihood that something will eventually get said, that there is something to wait for. It was nothing like that with her. With her it was always silence, never even the far-off misty vista of a reply. And her face was always the same, too. She smiled faintly like the statue of a moderately well-disposed goddess, except that she was made of flesh, not marble, and wore not a himation but a black blazer over a white skirt.

"Do you have any idea how many times this has happened? It's scores, a hundred. I'll be, say, in a canoe with a friend—Ben Hirsch, say—paddling down a river on a bright October day. We'll pass by some people picnicking on the bank and you'll be among them. Or I'll be in some interminable meeting, the kind where people are too bored to object to anything, when the droning vice president of this or that or other reads his own slides, bullet-points running down the screen as if put there with a Tommy gun, and I'll catch sight of you sitting at the far end of the conference table, serene as always. Or I'll be in the middle of the deciding set of a championship match on a stifling July afternoon and, when I change sides, I'll spot you up among the spectators, cool even in that blazer. I've endured this for eleven years. You're in the next room; you're at the stove; you're in a crowd on the subway. You never have anything to do with what's going on but there you are, getting into a car across a street or walking down the pavement holding a cup of coffee. I admit it's always a thrill to see you, but it's stimulation without consolation and so no comfort at all. Worst still were the two sexual encounters. Remember them? For me, they were exciting and frustrating, like clutching at a cloud. What were they for you?"

The affair had lasted six years. She was married, not unhappily enough, and he had become divorced after the first year. She had two children; he had zero. As they were a secret from everyone else, they had no secrets from each other. Through all those years, the happiest of his life, he accepted his position at the bottom of her priority list and resigned himself to the trips they couldn't take, the nights they couldn't spend together. But then she began to make excuses for putting off their trysts. He pined and felt humiliated by the undeniable one-sidedness. He was unhappy and felt his dignity draining away. She wants to end it, he thought, but doesn't know how or hasn't the courage. And so, when she phoned to put off one more of their afternoons without even bothering to give a reason, he erupted, not with anger but out of pain. He hadn't planned it. In fact, he was stunned by what came out of his mouth. The tone was all wrong and what he said didn't in the least reflect the emotions he felt. It came out like a cost-benefit analysis.

"Look, do you want to end things?" he concluded and knew at once that her answer might destroy him. She was silent. What had he done? He waited as long as he could but there was nothing. The silence provoked him and, without willing it, he filled the void the only way he could. "I can't do this anymore," he blurted. "It's not because I don't love you; it's because I can't stop. And I have to try." She didn't hang up. There was only more silence, a silence which never went away.

Now, all these years later, after all her wordless cameo appearances in his dreams, he confronted that silence. He was in a park on a cloudy, warm afternoon. It felt like a Sunday in late summer. People were walking dogs, wrangling toddlers, tossing balls, riding bikes, holding hands. He was on his way to a softball game. He was the second baseman.

A bag with his spikes, glove, and a bottle of water hung from his hand. He was late and hurrying. Out of the corner of his eye, he saw her seated alone on a bench. He had never done it before, never approached. He never felt that he had that much control. He thought it was against the rules. If he had ever tried before—at the tennis match, at the meeting—he couldn't remember doing so. Maybe he had woken up the moment he took the first step toward her. But now, for some reason, it was possible. He sat himself down beside her and dropped the bag between his feet. Though he said little, it felt like he spoke for whole days and nights.

He took a deep breath. "There's been no one else," he said to her marmoreal profile. "Maybe if you took yourself out of my unconscious, stopped stealing around my prefrontal cortex, gave up playing the returning repressed, maybe then I could find somebody else. Perhaps it's not too late. So, I'm begging you. Go away. Stay away."

And she moved. Without altering her expression, that comforting and tormenting smile, she turned toward him, raised her hand, and lightly brushed his cheek with the back of her hand. It was like the gentlest of slaps. Her fingers were warm.

He woke in a derangement of feeling. She had touched him and he was happy to have been near her; but as the sweet, painful sensation faded from his unshaven cheek, he shuddered into consciousness, certain that he would have to go on being alone.

2. La Moulante - *Concertino en do majeur pour flûte et cordes, élastique et vif à la fin*

When Pierre Brunelle first set foot in the city on a stupefyingly tropical afternoon eight months earlier, there was still rubble to be seen, especially in Bellefleur, the district with which he had professionally to do. What the locals called the Great Trembling had struck four years earlier. The quake took a fearful toll in lives and a catastrophic one in property. Bellefleur was a poor neighborhood and so had the most irresponsible construction. The three-story tenements characteristic of the district had collapsed on their residents like the fist of a smiting Judge. In fact, according to his client, Monsieur Foisanant, that was exactly what more than one of the local clergy declared the quake to be.

"It is not an enlightened country," he had said drily as if the citizens had indeed been punished but for the sin of ignorance—perhaps for believing in sin.

Pierre did not feel so scornful. He understood that the wish to moralize a disaster is as natural as the calamity itself, however mistaken.

The two men sat in Bruenelle's small, modern office in the Onzième Arrondisement which did not shake at all.

"Haven't you noticed that a bad turn of luck can feel like a chastisement?" said Pierre. He smiled to soften the disagreement. "People like to find a meaning in things, especially bad ones."

Foisanant grunted. "The Bellefleur district was leveled," he said brutally, "and that, for me, is its meaning. I picked up a huge chunk of it for a song. And that, assuming we can come to terms, is where you will build. I want luxury apartments—four floors of them—above one of commercial space and three for offices. The city got a lot of aid and it's rebuilding. Plenty of new infrastructure. I'm betting the place has a future."

"But Monsieur Foisonant, I've done some research. There are laws restricting the height of buildings to only three floors. You are asking for seven."

Foisanant sat back in the soft leather chair; Pierre sat up straight on the hard one provided for clients. He tapped his fingers together with an air of satisfaction. "That's been seen to," he said.

Bribes, thought Pierre.

"Besides," Foisanant continued, "*my* researches tell me another quake is improbable, that it'll most likely be decades before the plates shift again. I have it from an expert, a professor."

"Most likely?" said Pierre.

Foisanant shrugged. "All of life is a matter of probabilities. We take automobiles for granted, but how probable was a Renault Clio or a Volkswagen Golf calculated from the Big Bang?"

Pierre had no idea what to say to this.

"Now, to the point. I chose you to design the building for me because you're young, unmarried and so easy to relocate, and you enjoy a good reputation, though hardly yet a great one. As construction costs will be low, especially wages, I'm giving you carte blanche to come up with something that will make your name, mine—and get into the tonier magazines. It goes without saying that I want you to make it as safe as you can, Brunelle. Within reason, naturally."

"Within reason?"

"Not to worry. I'll make sure that it's well insured."

Despite his misgivings, Pierre signed the contract. Foisanant's insurance policy would cover the building, not the people inside of it. Now that he was on the spot, had seen the city and looked over the site, his compunction was hardly allayed—on the contrary.

He took an apartment near the city center. It was low-ceilinged but large and very cheap, big enough for an office that could accommodate his whole staff and with spacious living quarters for himself. The climate was oppressive. He arranged for two air-conditioners and a generator. Power cuts, like beggars, muggings, and heavily armed police were commonplace in the city.

Pierre's design was informed by a thoroughgoing review of the work of those few architects he admired; that is, the most imaginative and forward-looking. Yet the plan he had devised was original. In contrast to the rundown, post-colonial look of the city, his building would be in a style he privately thought of as neo-neo-classical. And yet, after a week in the place, he reconsidered. His seven-floors, he realized, had been thought up in Paris, in the abstract, without context, as if he were going to erect them over thin air. He begged Foisanant to put off his deadline for a month and began making modifications. The building would still stand out, just less like a sore thumb.

Pierre preferred the open stalls to the well-stocked hygienic supermarket that served well-to-do and expatriates. He did his shopping early, before the heat of the day, and sometimes lingered to watch the country people unloading produce from pickup trucks, donkey carts, mopeds, even bicycles. Two outsized canvas awnings covered the stalls. He admired the simplicity and precise spacing of the wooden supports. The poles were set into round metal fittings hammered into the beaten earth. One morning, as he stood in their shade, the awnings began to flutter oddly, as if caught in contrary gusts. Then he felt the tremor beneath his feet. Everybody froze. The tremor was slight and lasted only seconds, yet Pierre wished Foisanant's professor had been on hand to feel it.

"We're going to change the plans again," he announced to his team an hour later. Those who were French emitted Gallic groans; the locals looked pleased. For the former, this meant more time away from home and, for the latter, the chance of more weeks of employment.

"What is it?" asked Alaire, his first assistant.

"You didn't feel it?"

"What?"

"The earthquake, of course."

"Earthquake? No." Alaire looked at the others. They all shrugged except his secretary Lucille, a laconic local. "It was tiny," she said in a voice to match. "Nothing. Ordinary."

Pierre obsessed over the problem of how to make his building earthquake-proof—within reason. Firm up the foundation? Buttresses? He remembered the poles in the market. Could he sink girders into the bedrock of Bellefleur? He couldn't see how any of these measures would succeed.

The problem was driving him crazy. He also had to consider Foisanant's deadline. He'd already asked for a second delay and, to put it mildly, Foisanant didn't agree with a good grace. Pierre found sleeping difficult, even with the air-conditioner. He did experience the pleasant exhaustion that comes after a day of achievement but the dispiriting sort one gets from accomplishing nothing. When his client phoned demanding a progress report, he tried to explain.

"I'm afraid there's going to be another earthquake, maybe another big one. A building with seven floors will be a deathtrap."

"Didn't I tell you to do your best?"

"Yes, you did."

"Well, have you?"

"Not yet."

"No more delays, Brunelle. Get on with it."

Toward morning, Pierre fell into a fitful sleep and had a dream, a happy one that took him back home and to his childhood. He was in the garden behind his grandparents' country house in Senlis. There was to be a big family picnic. The high-summer afternoon was perfect, everything green and lush. The blue hydrangea blooms were the size of footballs. His aunt and uncle had come early with his favorite cousin, Henriette. They were of an age. He wanted to play croquet. Henriette agreed and he began setting up the wickets.

"Oh," said his cousin. "Wait a minute. There's something I want to show you."

"What?"

"Just wait."

Henriette ran to her parents' car and returned holding a colorful little cube.

"What's that?"

"My friend Cecile brought it back for me from America."

Pierre felt impatient. He wanted to get to the croquet. "Well, let's see it, then."

"Come over to the steps."

"Just show me now," he demanded.

"Oh, very well."

Henriette opened the box and took out a metal cylinder. She tossed it into the air. It uncoiled and fell straight back into her grasp.

"It can walk down steps!" she crowed.

Pierre awoke and dashed into the office, to his drawing board.

"Yes. Yes, it's possible," he muttered to himself. "If I isolate the base, it can be done."

He sketched a rough design for four large springs and how they could be anchored to the foundation and reinforced with tensile steel. It was an entirely original idea, the kind that would save lives and make its inventor famous.

"Henriette's toy!" Who'd have thought? he shouted then laughed out loud.

3. Rêves Prophétiques - *Symphonie pour deux orchestres en modes Phrygien et Lydien, lascive et belliqueuse*

At dawn, Bordeaux lay quiet below the castle of Roquetaillade. Guillaume stood on the battlements breathing in the still smoke-free air.

He was no longer the frank and hopeful youth who had assumed the title of Duke of Aquitaine a decade before but a harder man of thirty-two, more inclined to suspicion than trust. A half-hour earlier, he had awakened from a terrible dream. Like his contemporaries, Guillaume believed in Heaven, Hell, Purgatory, Limbo, and the Nicene Creed. He also believed that dreams are true revelations, though of what isn't always clear. He couldn't be sure if his dream revealed what had happened, what would happen, or what might happen.

He had wakened in a fury. His first impulse was to march to his wife's chamber, dismiss her ladies, shake her awake and demand to know if she'd been unfaithful. But he had learned caution. Brisca was from a powerful family that traced itself back to the time of Hugh Capet. Guillaume's marriage, which until that morning he had thought a happy one, was also an indispensable alliance. His mother-in-law had never liked him; she considered him an upstart. Rage and prudence jousted in his brain.

Two months earlier, Guillaume had entertained his neighboring ruler, Odo, Duke of Gascony, a man eight years his junior but two years older than Brisca. Feeding and housing Odo and his entourage for three weeks had been costly, but the agreements they negotiated justified the expense. Now Guillaume reviewed the episodes of that state visit. How had Odo and Brisca behaved toward one another? Always properly, so far as he knew, with formal courtesy and nothing more. But three weeks was a long time, enough for the exchange of glances and messages, for trysts.

In one sense, the dream was not obscure. In it, he had been concealed behind an arras in Brisca's chamber. On her high bed, Odo was gyrating atop of his wife whose moans of pleasure were of a sort he had never heard.

As the sun rose and the town began to stir, victory in the joust fell to anger, fortified by jealousy. Yet Guillaume was still chary of acting precipitously at least with respect to his wife. He decided against confronting her and instead started to plan an attack on Gascony aimed at hacking Odo to pieces. He could have it out with Brisca afterwards.

Summoned to Bordeaux by discreet couriers, the lords of Aquitaine gathered in what they were surprised to find was a council of war.

"But, My Lord, we understood your meeting with Duke Odo went smoothly," said the Marquis of Torny, at fifty the most senior man there.

"Not as smoothly as all that," Guillaume retorted. "How many men can you muster in a month, Torny?"

The same question was put to them all.

"No word of this meeting must get abroad. We'll gather in secret."

Once again, the Marquis of Torny spoke up. "There's to be no declaration?"

His implication was clear, that a surprise attack was dishonorable.

Guillaume frowned. "No," he said firmly. "I'm informed that Odo is in the north, in Auch. This is convenient. We can take the town before he moves his court south to Torbes." He looked hard at Torny, who said nothing more but gave a slight bow.

"There will be two columns. I'll lead the larger and you, Marquis, will command the other."

There was no need to point out that this meant a larger share of land and loot.

"As you wish, My Lord."

Guillaume motioned for the Marquis to draw closer. "Good," he whispered. "The others look to you. As to the reason for the war, I'll explain that to you later, in private. You must promise to keep it to yourself."

A month later, the two columns with their mounted knights, archers, and ranks of pikemen crossed the frontier. Guillaume's was to march along the east bank of the Garonne, Torny's on the west in order to cut off any possibility of Odo fleeing toward Torbes.

Where the Garonne joined the River Gers lay some high cliffs. On their way to Auch, Guillaume's column had the Gers to their left and these cliffs to the right. A light rain was falling when they reached the spot late in the morning. As Guillaume's column proceeded under the cliffs, huge boulders suddenly rolled down on them followed by a storm of arrows. This onslaught was followed by infantry streaming up from the south behind a vanguard of heavy cavalry. In the mêlée, a lucky bolt from a crossbow pierced the eyehole of Gullaume's plumed and burnished helmet. Observing all this from the eastern bank, the Marquis of Torny at once ordered his column back to Aquitaine and the rout was on.

The Dukedom, reduced in extent by the victorious Odo, passed to the half-brother of Brisca, which greatly pleased her mother. Guillaume's widow retained her title and willingly accepted her mother's advice not to remarry.

Some years later, the Marquis of Torny, now a very old man and trusted advisor to the new duke, was invited to the wedding of Odo's son to the daughter of the Count of Guînes. He attended with some misgivings but was received warmly and with dignity. After the wedding feast, Torny had a page take a message to Duke Odo asking for a brief audience. The page returned promptly.

"My Lord says it would be a pleasure to meet with you, Monsieur le Marquis. Please follow me."

The conversation was brief.

"Guillaume was very careful," said Torny. "How did you discover his plans? A spy, I presume?"

Odo smiled and took a sip of wine. "You know, I've never told anyone about that. It's true, I knew he intended to attack me at Auch. I even knew about the two columns."

"Did you know one of them was mine?"

Odo's eyebrows went up. "No, I didn't. The one that escaped, obviously."

The Marquis inclined his head.

"Well," said Odo, "it was through a dream. In this dream, I was standing on the heights above the Gers. I could see the two columns on either side of the river. I spotted Guillaume's pennant and made my plans."

On his return to Bordeaux, the Marquis went to see the widowed Duchess and told her the whole story.

"There's something I would like to ask you, My Lady."

"Yes?"

"By any chance, did you too have a dream?"

Brisca replied with a little laugh. "Oh, I never remember my dreams. They always fly away like smoke the moment I wake up. Does that happen to you, too, My Lord?"

Lost City

The sun had just touched the steppe when we climbed out of the Land Rovers, beating dust off our clothes in gestures that had become second nature. Our shadows stretched up a low heap of rubble. Because of the rosy light, the damage looked fresh, as though the city had been razed a mere six hours and not six centuries before.

Krueger squatted down and picked up a pebble. "Right where you're supposed to be," he said addressing either the stone in his hand or the whole hillock of gravel.

The last week had humbled even Krueger. He didn't crow about his navigation; on the contrary, he spoke as if the city were to be congratulated for not having relocated.

We could tell he was moved and so the rest of us held our tongues. This was his moment of triumph and anyway the steppe had abraded our enthusiasm. Nice for Krueger, we thought, but we were disappointed and weary down to our dendrites. Though he had promised us nothing more than this tumescence of debris, who could have helped hoping for something richer, grander, stranger? After all, the phrase *lost city* excites the imagination.

On the far side of the rubble, halfway up a swale, we could see four huts and a couple cultivated plots marked out by stones. Nothing was moving over there, not even a goat.

"That's a surprise," somebody said. We had grown used to seeing the black tents and beshitted flocks of the nomads whose paths we occasionally crossed but nothing resembling those huts.

"Suppose we could get a beer over there?" said Krueger. And, to raise our spirits, we laughed.

The light was dying as we picked our way gingerly over the ruins. It was impossible to make any sense of them; that is, to see them as an ex-city. Where once, according to Krueger, there had been an ornate mosque, four wide boulevards, a marketplace, cisterns and gardens, now there was nothing at all. Not so much as two bricks together, no trace of the thick walls that were supposed to have surrounded but failed to protect the place. The destruction had been methodical and thorough. Modern artillery is haphazard by comparison. Even a bombed-out city is still the skeleton of a city; you can make out where the streets, the foundations were. The pulverizing here had been retail, not wholesale.

We made camp by the Rovers and ate a meal of corned beef hash. Our mood was subdued.

Krueger had organized the trip, promising us a kind of working escape, a vacation adventure. He called us, the most bored of his college chums, sold us on the idea, pried a couple thousand dollars out of each of us and eked out the expenses with an advance on his photographs and a small grant from some foundation where his wife has contacts. His plan was to retrace a forgotten trade route in central Asia, a spur of the famous Silk Road. We traveled from west to east, picked up the Rovers in Germany and stopped well short of the Chinese frontier. Krueger had it all worked out. We could pack everything we needed, he said. Language would be no problem, as he spoke fluent Russian and, if we needed to trade with the nomads, signs would serve. He had a pretty good idea of where the city was and reckoned it would take about three weeks to get there, allowing for a little searching, and no more than a couple more to get back. The site was somewhere in the middle of a blank space on the map suggestively named the Hunger Steppe.

According to Krueger, even in its halcyon days Suzam-Ord had never been exactly a metropolis, probably no more than a couple thousand people. For a few decades, though, it had been fabulously affluent. Then, a Mongol khan, who was busy pillaging up north, sent three messengers down to the city demanding a token tribute, routine business for the time. But the caliph of Suzam-Ord, despising the nomadic infidels and puffed up with hubris, beheaded the messengers. For two years nothing happened, and Suzam-Ord rolled on, fat and happy. Then one morning the city awoke to find barbarians on its doorstep, ferocious, foul-smelling men on fierce, tiny horses. They took the city, slaughtered its citizens, sealed up its springs, razed every edifice to the ground. Before riding off. the Khan is supposed to have laid a curse on the place for good measure. After that the caravans stayed away and Suzam-Ord vanished from the maps and pretty much from memory.

Krueger had read all this in an old manuscript he got from some professor pal of his wife's. He unrolled a copy of the manuscript then poured us each a glass of vodka and we drank to the discovery of Suzam-Ord. Why not? We had all looked up to Krueger in the old days. He had been our motivator, our idea-man. He organized our parties, persuaded us to go to Mardi Gras, scrounged tickets to *Hair*, bought the beat-up Chevy that got us to Fort Lauderdale and half the way back. Now he had rescued us from the ennui of our careers, the monotony of our marriages. Why shouldn't we follow him, even now, even to Suzam-Ord? No doubt we had rescued him as well. Krueger was hyperkinetic, couldn't bear idleness; he was the sort of man who takes improbable vacations and looks over your shoulder at parties.

We awoke at first light to find Krueger already at the top of the rubble snapping photographs.

"The ruins at dawn," he cried down to us cheerfully.

"What ruins?" we yelled back, rubbing our eyes.

Considering the unmitigated emptiness that stretched to the horizon it was hard to believe there had ever been enough here to support even a small town. Yet there must still have been a trickle of water that escaped the Khan's seals, enough to sustain those little gardens over by the huts.

"How long are we going to stay here?" one of us asked.

Krueger made a dismissive motion with his arm as he peered through his camera, clicked, then shrugged. "We can head back tomorrow."

This was welcome news. We had had an uneasy night. It wasn't quite homesickness we felt, and it wasn't superstition, but it was something. None of us mentioned the story of the curse; nevertheless, there was no denying the place had a bad feeling about it. We had grown more or less accustomed to the vacancy of the steppes, but this was something else. The utter destruction, the finality of it, the story of massacre, perhaps all that made us sleep badly and gave us bad dreams.

Once he had all the pictures, he wanted Krueger suggested we go over to the huts.

"What for? There's obviously nobody there."

Krueger looked at us over his beard. "Hey, we're explorers. Remember?"

It wasn't yet nine o'clock, but it was already hot. We preferred walking around the ruins rather than trying to pick our way over the debris. The sun would have heated the stones and anyway it was safer; nothing easier than to lose your footing on a pile like that.

The huts turned out to be ramshackle affairs of lath and tarpaper, but they were reinforced against the wind and weather with milled two-by-fours and strips of metal. The roofs were corrugated tin.

The first hut had a proper wooden door off which grey paint was flaking. Krueger knocked three times.

We waited, expecting nothing. But then the door was opened by an ancient fellow who looked like a Tartar though he greeted us in proper Russian. He wore a polo shirt and shorts and invited us to come in. "Welcome. Would you care for some tea?"

Krueger answered him, then translated for us. "He said welcome and would we care for some tea." We filed in behind him.

Another man was seated at a card table, and he looked even older than the first one. Eight folding chairs were scattered around the single room. The old fellow at the card table nodded at us with energy but said nothing. The younger one, though, made a little speech.

"We saw you arrive last evening," said our host. "Forgive us for not coming to welcome you to our city but, as you see, we are a little debilitated. Please make yourselves comfortable."

We arranged the chairs in a semi-circle.

"Where are you from?"

Krueger spoke for us. "We're Americans, from the United States."

"Ah," said the old man without evincing much surprise. "Sooner or later Americans go everywhere, to the moon and even here. Like your Lewis and Clark," he chuckled.

Krueger was amazed and he translated. The crack about Lewis and Clark astonished the rest of us too. Krueger asked the old man why he called the place his city.

"Because this *is* our city. We belong to it," the old man answered with a serene Asiatic smile.

"I don't understand," said Krueger.

A faint whistle issued from the teapot. Our host motioned for his silent companion to see to it and when the old man made a face at him our host gently raised a finger.

Then the door opened, and two more human antiquities shambled in. Unlike our host, who stood upright, they were stooped. One was wearing a Chicago Cubs cap. When he heard that we were Americans he had to shake all our hands and laughed as if this were a terrific joke.

He kept pointing to his cap and nodding. "Cups," he said. "Never win."

The other newcomer was less voluble but managed a bitter little speech, quickly translated by Krueger. "Welcome to Suzam-Ord, once the diamond of the steppe and the wonder of Asia, now a corpse lying on a dry mattress."

The others scowled at him.

We were each handed a glass containing about two fingers of some kind of tea, massively sugared.

Three more old men showed up. More nodding and smiles. It seemed everybody had something to say. It was awkward for Krueger to keep translating and he pretty much gave up. More tea was brewed, more chairs occupied. The overcrowded hut was soon overheated as well. Krueger fell into deep conversation with three of the old men and apparently forgot about us. Our host did most of the talking. The others had a lot to say too but less to Krueger than to each other. Their speeches grew longer, more emphatic and, apparently, polemical. Eventually they gave up addressing Krueger at all and began arguing with one another. Kreuger took out his notebook and a pencil.

After fifteen minutes of this we were all bored and dripping with sweat.

"For God's sake, it's stifling. Let's get out of here," one of us whispered.

"Come on, Krueger, we're taking off."

"What?"

"We're dying in here. And we don't know what they're arguing about. Let's go."

He motioned indifferently for us to leave and turned back to listen.

As soon as we got to our feet everybody fell silent, embarrassed.

Then Krueger stood up and made some excuse for us, but we weren't permitted to leave until we had shaken hands all around. Krueger stayed.

"Maybe they're ghosts," one of us joked on the way back to camp.

"Oh sure. A ghost with a Cubs cap."

"Caretakers then?"

"Of what? Gravel?"

"Hey, what do you suppose those codgers were going on about?"

"Maybe the prudence of leaving heads on strangers."

"Odd, wasn't it?"

"What?"

"That business about this being *their* city."

"Well, old men. You know."

"*Really* old. They all looked at least ninety."

"Everything dries out here."

While we waited for Krueger to return, we checked our gear for the ride back and then played poker for the Cuban cigars we'd picked up in Poland. We loved those cigars. It became a postprandial ritual for us each night. Tobacco was sacred. We puffed and talked with more candor as the trip went on.

Somebody asked if we ought to go check on Krueger. We made jokes about the old men being the last survivors of the Golden Horde, bloodless after half a millennium but still bloodthirsty. Then we returned to our game.

Krueger sauntered in around mid-afternoon, red and sweaty as if he'd been in a sauna. We had plenty of questions, but he said what we were asking was a little crude and promised to read us his notes after dinner. "I tried to get down everything I could," he explained. "I wrote it out as if it was just a monologue. I couldn't keep the speakers straight."

"So, they didn't even *try* to cut your head off?"

Krueger made a face and drank a whole bottle of water. "After dinner, okay? Give me a little time to rehydrate and look this stuff over."

"Okay. We'll eat early, then. Chili and rice and the last of that Montrachet."

On the steppe, the temperature drops like a guillotine at night; the sky evaporates, and you feel like you're floating through space. The stars are infinite yet near and we felt like a band of astronauts.

Seeing how it was our last night before turning back, Krueger broke out a bottle of Remy-Martin after coffee. We didn't know he'd been keeping it. Then he sat himself next to the lantern and read his notes to us. Later, after we had returned home, he mailed us each a spruced-up copy.

"We were all born in a village twenty kilometers to the east of the city. Everyone in our village was descended from the few who escaped from Suzam-Ord. The story the survivors was passed down to us. They hid under dead bodies for two days waiting for the horsemen to leave. They scraped a living from the steppe through small farming and trading with the nomads, to whom they sold some of their daughters. Always our fathers kept the memory of Suzam-Ord alive, even maintaining something of its traditions too, though in a fitful and deformed fashion. We had no Koran, only a few verses that the boys all had to learn by heart:

So, when the trumpet is blown with a single blast
and the earth and the mountains are lifted up and
crushed with a single blow,
then, on that day, the terror shall come to pass,
and heaven shall be split, for upon that day it shall be very frail. . . .

"And that's how life was for generations until it was disrupted by the Revolution, then collectivization, finally by the Great Patriotic War. All of us boys were of fighting age when the war broke out and, when we learned of it, we met together and decided to volunteer all together. We were in late teens and full of dreams, sick to death of our village, fed up with the steppe and poverty. This is how we became good Soviet men, men of the future. We fought for four years, though not in the same unit. We survivors didn't want to come back. We stayed on in Russia and started families and were sure we were free of the past. Not one of us told his wife or children about Suzam-Ord. We were ashamed of our ancestors. They were backward and for generations clung to the tatters of a vanishing religion and memories of a dead city. They were superstitious. We believed we had gone well beyond them, that we had slogged through the horrors of war into a new dawn, free of curses and prophecies. Without us, without its young men, the village died. The population drifted off—to the nomads or into Siberia, who knows where?

"One May Day a bunch of us ran into each another in a parade of veterans. We threw our arms around each others' necks, overcome with emotion. We resolved to see if others from our village had also survived. It took two years for us to find each other. We exchanged letters, then made visits on holidays. Maybe it is only the nature of old men, but the more decrepit we grew the more the old ways seemed to reassert themselves and the more the new ways that had appeared strong as steel began to dissolve. We found ourselves talking about Suzam-Ord and our fathers who had said that the city would be reborn when the curse was laid. Perhaps, we began to think, it is up to us, up to us to lay that curse. After all, who else was there to do it?

"How much did we actually believe? Well, it would not be misleading to say none of us believed with a whole heart. But even a provisional, far-fetched faith was better than the emptiness we all felt. Perhaps you too have felt this need? What else could have made you and your friends travel halfway around the world just to look at that poor pile of stones over there? It's hardly attractive, our quintessence of nothingness in the middle of the steppe. I don't say that you share our longing, but you may at least sympathize with it. I imagine that for an American such yearnings express themselves in motion. Isn't it true that you dream of riding into the West and never stopping? No doubt as a people you are still too young to feel what six centuries of irrationality and stasis mean. Well, we too felt restless. For us, though, the way lay to the East.

"Now we are all here, without our wives, our children and grandchildren. When we left, we told them our intentions and begged their pardon. We had to endure their tears, their worries, their anger, and at last their mockery. This was terrible, but we had each other. You too have your friends and will know their value, how they bear you up, even when they argue with you.

"As for us, we miss our families and we argue all the time. Everything is a matter for dispute, everything. To argue has become, in a sense, our calling. Perhaps, if we were young enough, we might actually try to rebuild our city. But, as you see, we are too old and too few. Our lives have given us many experiences and opinions, therefore with much to disagree about. Above all, though, we disagree about Suzam-Ord. For example, some of us say they believe in the prophecy that the city will again become great; a few go so far as to claim that it is destined to become the center of an empire extending to the Banda Sea. Others believe in the prophecy too but more modestly; they think that the city will someday be rebuilt and that this rebuilding itself will lift the curse. The curse itself is a great cause of dispute among us because no one knows its exact nature. A few of us don't believe in it and say it was just a Mongol trick to keep trade away. Others say not only that there is a curse but that to remove it will require some special sacrifice. Three beheadings, for example, to make up for those of the khan's emissaries. Oh yes, last night there was even some talk about you and two of your friends in this regard. No, please don't be alarmed! I assure you that this proposal came from the very smallest of minorities, and even he was really just making a joke, though in the way men joke about holy things. Anyway, others believe the curse and the prophecy to be tied together so that one implies the other. They wish to believe in the one for the sake of the other. Underneath this wishful believing, however, is the apprehension that there is no curse to expiate and no prophecy to be fulfilled, that the only truths are the dictates of geography and the unrepeatable events of history. Geography is obviously against us, while politics and commerce have long ago passed Suzam-Ord by. If we were to credit only facts, we would have to admit our city is dead three times over, that it is impossible to build even the humblest of expectations on this stony ground. You can see that for yourself. Yet some have an answer even for this. They argue that because time moves in cycles every past is bound to become some future, as the present will soon be that past and, again, a still more distant future. The most pious of us argues that our best course lies in silence, practical activity, and fulfilling the commandment for daily prayers. He declares that everything lies in the hands of Allah.

"Well, who knows? Perhaps Allah does watch over the steppe and long ago counted up every pebble in Suzam-Ord. Where one has faith in nothing it becomes easy to believe anything. If, after all we have seen with our own eyes, even one of us can believe then why shouldn't we all? Why shouldn't the city even be rebuilt? With Him everything is possible. It is even possible that you and your friends have come here as Allah's instruments. The world, we know, is changing. What we thought was history, what we thought were our true lives, turns out merely to have been history holding its breath. We have come back to die. Why shouldn't our city come back to life?

"The steppe is a lonesome place. It is hard to put down roots here. Only the nomads are truly at home on the steppe because they are always on the move. A city on the steppe, isn't it an absurdity? And yet there once was such a city. And here we are, we and you together, because of this city.

"We are content to end our days in each other's company and to be buried here on the steppe, beside our city. May the emptiness of our lives may be improved by the fullness of our deaths."

It's been more than a year now, plenty of time for us all to get back in harness, steeped in the routines of our lives. Even Krueger seems finally to have settled down. We don't keep in close touch, just a phone call from time to time. Everyone says he's fine, family doing well, work going all right. We make jokes about the ready availability of lettuce and oranges and if any of us smoke cigars we smoke them in solitude, on the deck, beside the barbecue. We are all clean shaven, take regular showers, and everything that happens to us is in accord with normal laws. We feel only what one ought to feel. Our sleep is untroubled.

Hsi-wei and the Mogwai

In early autumn, when the trees had yet to lose their leaves, when skylarks and pipits were only beginning to migrate south, Chen Hsi-wei was making his way through Jizhou. The peasant/poet and itinerant maker of straw sandals was heading to Taiyuan, a large town where he hoped to buy an inkstone, a new brush, and two or three small scrolls. His supply of cash being, to put it mildly, negligible, he set up his sign in the villages he encountered along the way soliciting customers. The nights were still warm enough that he could economize by sleeping in the open.

He arrived in the village of Anshun shortly after noon and went straight to the communal well. It was by a wall which formed one side of the town square. There were some stalls offering local produce, household goods, bolts of cloth, and two old women with braziers selling dumplings. Everyone took note of the stranger. A few looked with interest, most with suspicion. One of the old women nodded at His-wei; it might have been a sign of welcome or perhaps in hope of a sale. He gave her a little bow and a shrug.

Hsi-wei leaned his sign against the wall.

The best season for selling straw sandals is, of course, spring when peasants need a fresh pair. But the end of summer is next best because some will want replacements on hand for the coming year, and parents will need new sandals for children who have outgrown their old ones.

Hsi-wei took a few orders, mostly for children. Small sandals require as much work as large ones but he always charged less. An old man, who smiled when told the price, ordered three pairs for his grandchildren. He took a length of string from his jacket and, with a small knife, cut three pieces. "That's about how big their soles are," he said. He handed Hsi-wei the strings then held out his hand to seal the bargain.

"A good price," he said. "My name's Chen. In my time, I've worn out I don't know how many sandals. I'm seventy years old."

Hsi-wei took the old man's hand. "My name's also Chen and I'm exactly half your age."

Though the empire was as chockful of Chens as of Wangs, Fengs, and Zhous, the old peasant had to find out if they were related.

Hsi-wei told Mr. Chen that he had been born in a village near the capital, Daxing.

"Ah," said Mr. Chen, "then probably not. But," he added with a twinkle in his eyes, "you never know."

"Has your family always lived here?"

"As far as I know we Chens have been here since the Qin Dynasty—maybe even before that."

"Do you like it here in Anshun?"

The old man looked surprised by the question. "Like it? But it's home."

"Is life hard?"

"That depends on the weather—and the landlords."

"Are there many landlords here?

"There are three, but two hardly count. Most of the land belongs to the Fei family, even after the Emperor's reforms."

"Are the Feis good landlords?"

"The old one, Fei Caishan, was good. If there was a flood, he forgave half the rent, and during the terrible drought ten years back, he canceled all of it."

"Then there is a new landlord?"

The old man nodded and frowned. “Caishan’s younger brother, Fei Hao. No sooner did he take over than he raised everybody’s rent. We miss Caishan.”

“Did the old landlord die of sickness?”

“No. It’s four years since he was fished out of the river. They said he tripped, hit his head on a piling, fell in and drowned. That’s what we were told.”

“You don’t believe that’s what happened?”

Mr. Chen looked around, drew close and whispered. “The story could be true. The magistrate swallowed it. But who hits his head on a piling and drowns?”

Hsi-wei asked Mr. Chen where he could get some good straw and, with the thought of finding a cheap place to work and bed down, whether the local tavern had a stable.

Mr. Chen smiled. “You need straw and a place to sleep?”

“I do.”

Mr. Chen smiled cannily. “Well, sandal-maker, I can offer both, if you’re not fussy about sleeping next to a pig pen and you’ll make one of the pairs of sandals free.” Hsi-wei accepted the offer and spent the night at Chen’s cottage working on his sandals and sleeping for a few hours.

The next day Hsi-wei returned to the town square working at his orders and securing two more. He noticed a slim, well-dressed woman at the stall that sold cloth. She kept turning to stare at him. At last, she came over. Up close, the woman appeared careworn.

Hsi-wei got to his feet. “How can I help you, My Lady?”

The woman examined Hsi-wei uncertainly. “This may seem an odd question, but do you know a poem called ‘Yellow Moon at Lake Weishan’?”

"I do," Hsi-wei replied, wondering, not for the first time, whether other sandal-makers had been asked a similar question.

"How about the one people call 'Letter to Yang Jian'?"

"Yes, My Lady, I know that as well."

"Oh. And might your name be Chen? Chen Hsi-wei?"

"It is."

The woman's face lit up. "Are you the author of those poems?"

Hsi-wei made a modest bow.

"Oh! I was told that the poet was a sandal-maker, a peasant who travels all over, but I didn't believe it. Then it's really true?"

"As you see, My Lady. Would you like a pair of sandals?"

The woman who was wearing a fine pair of leather slippers smiled. "No," she said, "but I would be grateful if you would come to dinner tonight."

"Dressed like this?"

"Dressed however you like. My husband has been unwell of late, depressed, anxious, and morose. I worry about him. Perhaps you could cheer him up. He has little interest in poetry, but I occasionally read to him. When I read him your famous letter, he said it was a fine thing. His very words. A fine thing. It's been a long time since he said that about anything. Oh, I'm sorry. I ought to have introduced myself. I'm the wife of Fei Hao. My name is Yu-ming. Anshun is not large and our villa is nearby. It has two wings and a portico with four red pillars. The roof tiles are yellow. Just go down the road a quarter of a li and you'll see it. Will you come? Perhaps at sundown?"

Three hours later, Hsi-wei cleaned himself up with well water, put his sign and tools in his pack, and walked to the Fei villa. It was a large building. Its two-story wings were obviously additions to the older and more elegant building. An enclosed garden in the back was big enough for a pasture.

Fei Yu-ming welcomed him warmly and conducted him inside. The villa's furniture, like the building, was a mix of the antique and the new, old carved chairs, tables, and couches with many colorful new silk pillows.

Yu-ming summoned her husband. Fei Hao was less than enthusiastic about the arrival of his badly dressed guest but managed a stiff courtesy. He had the drawn and gloomy face of a man who did not relish his food, enjoy his garden, that of one who slept badly and who had shed weight.

"This is Chen Hsi-wei," said Yu-ming, "the poet."

"Yes. You told me he'd be coming to dinner."

Fei Hao ate little of the fine meal, which included both fish and pork courses, though he consumed a good deal of wine. He spoke little. The conversation was led by his wife, who tried hard to engage her husband in it.

"Hao, Master Hsi-wei tells me he was educated in Daxing. Remember how much you enjoyed your trip to the capital with Caishan all those years ago?"

Hao grunted. "Yes. My brother liked it there."

She reminded Fei of the poem he had said was fine then asked Hsi-wei to tell the story of the end of Yuchi. Hsi-wei explained that the ruthless bandit had been thrown down a well by peasants before the Emperor's cavalry caught up with him.

"Just what he deserved, and all because of your poem."

"I doubt that, My Lady."

"So do I," said Hao. "It seems unlikely that the poem led to the cavalry being sent to find him and the peasants dealing with him. I don't know much about poems, but it seems to me that most of them are about things that already happened, not what ought to happen. I liked that poem because of its power to make people indignant."

"And to bring about just punishment. I remember you saying that about it."

To this Hao said nothing.

After dinner, Yu-ming begged Hsi-wei to stay the night. Fei looked surprised then indifferent. "Our daughter Hua married years ago," explained his wife, "and our son Yuze is staying with his cousins in Shandang. We have many empty rooms. Why don't you men talk over the rest of the wine?" She looked pleadingly at Hsi-wei who said he was grateful for the invitation and would be pleased to spend some time with his host, if Fei wished it.

"Excellent!" said Yu-ming. "I'll show our guest to his room, Hoa, then send him back while I put it in order."

Hsi-wei followed Yu-ming into one of the villa's wings. As soon as they were out of earshot, she spoke hurriedly to Hsi-wei.

"You see what a state he's in. I believe it's the shock of his dear brother's death. Usually that kind of grief is sharp at first then lessens with time. But with Hao it's just the opposite. He was all right at first but now he's worse every day. Depressed, distracted. He takes pleasure in nothing. He's neglecting business, and I often find him just staring into space. I don't know what to do. Do you think you could help to raise his spirits?"

Hsi-wei felt pity for Yu-ming. "I've seen his condition, but I don't think I can alleviate it."

"Oh, do try. You are so good with words."

Hsi-wei returned to the dining room where Hao sat with his head in his hands before his cup and the wine jug. Without looking up, he said dully, resigned to his wife's whim, "We can sit in my study." He picked up the jug and motioned for Hsi-wei to bring their cups.

In the corridor, Hao came to a sudden halt, staggered, then looked furtively left and right.

"Are you all right, Mr. Fei?"

"Fine," he said, though fine is just what he did not look.

Hao's study was furnished more for comfort than work. There was a small desk beneath a shelf for scrolls, but the desk was empty and the shelf appeared too neat to have been in recent use. An upholstered couch and two old-fashioned armchairs, all piled high with pillows, provided seating. There was also a round table on which Hao deposited the wine jug before setting himself down on the couch with a loud groan and pointed to one of the chairs.

Plainly making a reluctant effort, Fei asked a question, though without sounding particularly eager to hear the answer. "So, Master Hsi-wei, cobbler and poet, peasant and scholar, how did you come to write that famous letter of yours?"

Hsi-wei examined Hao's face closely to judge the effect of his reply. "It was because of a ghost."

Fei looked almost alarmed.

"A ghost?"

"Yes. She visited me three times, always at night. Of course, I was probably just dreaming."

"Then you never saw the ghost during the day?"

"No. She told me she was one of those raped and slaughtered by Yuchi when he and his men attacked her village. She begged for justice and when I asked what I was to do, she told me to write a poem about Yuchi and to whom I should address it."

"Just a dream, then?"

"It's what I choose to believe."

"And yet you wrote the poem."

"As you know."

Fei was quiet for a moment. "It's strange," he said. "Strange that you would dream of this woman at all, let alone three times. Strange that she would come to you and strange that you would do what she asked."

"Not so strange, sir. I take my themes when they are given, and this is often in dreams. I suppose my mind made up the ghost and her plea by itself. Like many others, I had recently heard of Yuchi's outrages. And being a peasant, I shared the feelings of his helpless victims and the wish for justice."

"And for vengeance too?"

"Yes, that as well. And then too as a student I had read a version of the ancient legend of King Xuan of Zhou and his advisor Du Bo, the Duke of Tangdu. It is a story about haunting. Perhaps you know it?"

"No," said Fei, revealing his interest by leaning forward. "Look Master Chen, I haven't been sleeping well. My mother used to tell me stories at bedtime. Why don't you tell me this legend. Perhaps it will help me sleep."

"Very well," said Hsi-wei. "All this is said to have happened nearly a thousand years ago when Xuan became the eleventh king of the Zhou Dynasty after the Gong He regency. He restored central authority and dealt effectively with all his enemies both inside and outside his borders. Xuan appeared confident but he was superstitious and bridled at any challenge to the measures he took or the policies he announced. Like most superstitious people, he was quick to believe in prophecies and took seriously even improbable rumors."

“Prophecies may come true,” said Fei sententiously, “but rumors—rumors are poison. I’ve had to deal with them myself.”

“According to the story, King Xuan was confronted by both. One of his governors sent word of a rumor that a soothsayer in the Blue Mountains predicted a young woman would bring about the ruin of Jianshou, one the most prosperous town in the kingdom. The king summoned his generals at once and ordered the execution of all the young women not only in Jianshou but also the surrounding villages as well, more than a thousand, according to the legend. Xuan’s oldest, most loyal and upright advisor was the Duke Tangdu, Do Bu. He had been Xuan’s best commander during his war. They were like brothers. Do Bu happened to be in the chamber when Xuan issued his cruel decree. He stepped forward, kowtowed to the king, then got to his feet and spoke forthrightly. ‘I beg you to rescind this order. It is illogical, unjust, and unnecessary—wrong in every way. The prophecy—if there really was one—didn’t even say this dangerous woman would be found in Jianshou. It is abominable to kill innocent women on the strength of a rumor. Your decision does you no honor and will make you many enemies. Such an order is unworthy of the King of Zhou.’”

“Enraged, Xuan, ordered his guards to seize Do and lock him up.

“Toward dawn, the king had a dream. A hideous woman appeared. Her skin was green, which proved she was a demon. ‘I’ve come to warn you, Xuan. If you kill Do Bu, he will return to haunt you. Take heed.’

“The king awoke furious with Do Bu. He blamed the Duke of Tangdu, once his brother-in arms, for the nightmare and ordered his beheading before breakfast. The murders of a thousand women took a whole week. When his general reported the job done, Xuan felt no remorse; on the contrary, he felt relief and, of course, nobody ventured any criticism of his actions, not in public. Xuan’s kingdom was at peace, the frontiers secure; Jianshou was underpopulated but not destroyed, and life flowed untroubled for twelve months.

"According to the legend, exactly a year after the execution of Do Bu, King Xuan began to dream of him and, according to one version, actually to see him. At first, the ghost simply stood by the king's bed, staring at him balefully. This recurred night after night for another year. Like you, Mr. Fei, Xuan slept badly."

Hoa Fei made a frown and a fist. "What do you mean like me?" he demanded.

"But don't you remember telling me that you've not slept well of late?"

Fei relaxed his fist but not the frown. "Yes, that's so. Go on."

"So, King Xuan became irritable and melancholy. He spoke harshly to his ministers, guards, servants, wives, and concubines. He added new crimes and crueler punishments to his penal code. He raised taxes on both landlords and peasants. Then his visions became still worse. He saw—or imagined he saw—the ghost of Do Bu lurking in corners, behind pillars, in doorways. Do Bu spoke and always the same words: *illogical, unnecessary, unjust, abominable, unworthy.*'

"The king fell ill with a fever and his appetite deserted him. All the delicacies prepared to tempt him he found disgusting. The bad dreams and hallucinations persisted.

"On the last night of his life, King Xuan saw Do Bu at the foot of his bed. He held a bow and behind him stood a crowd of young women—red ones, orange ones, green, purple, and black. Do Bu spoke. 'Confess your error, make amends to the families of these poor women, humble yourself, give up your throne.'

"'Get away!' yelled the king so loudly that the guards burst in and, close behind them, his first wife.

"'What is it?' she cried.

"'Don't you see them?'

"'See who?'

"'Get away!' Xuan shouted again looking right through his wife and the guards. Then, focusing on his wife, he said more softly, 'It's nothing, only a dream. Go away.'

"As soon as the wife and guards had withdrawn, he again saw Do Bu and the thousand women. Do never took his eyes off the king. He reached behind him and took an arrow from the quiver on his back, placed it on the bow and shot it into Xuan's chest.

"In the morning, before breakfast, the king was found dead in his bed."

Fei looked pale. "It's a dreadful story."

"But only a story, just a legend."

"Then you don't believe in ghosts, that the dead can haunt the living? There are many stories about ghosts."

"Yes, stories. I don't believe in ghosts, but I do believe that the guilty see them in dreams, even in hallways and behind curtains."

Fei sank back on the couch. "It's late and I'm tired," he said peevishly.

Hsi-wei pointed to the jug. "But we haven't finished the wine."

"Never mind the wine, poet. Will you be leaving in the morning?"

"That's my intention, with gratitude for your generous hospitality."

Fei nodded and staggered to his feet.

By the time the household rose late in the morning, Hsi-wei had delivered his sandals and was already on the road to Taiyuan. Along with a note of gratitude, he left a poem for the Feis, the one people call 'The Mogwai.'

The spirits of the unjustly slain appear when
slowly falling flakes quiet the world,
on afternoons so sultry even the diligent leave work,
above the peonies in gardens, beneath the plum blossoms,
between courses when the guests are full of yellow wine.
But mostly it is at night that they stand by beds
hissing their rebukes, accusations, denunciations,
lurking in corners doorways, colonnades.

No one sees them skulking about save
those who cannot stop seeing them.

People say they can be mollified by burning money,
placated with prayers, assuaged by sacrifices.
They say these things the way mothers console children
as flood waters rise, the earth quakes and tiles fall,
when droughts bring famine that swell their bellies,
when ruthless bandits bellow through their villages;
but, like these, the mogwai are not to be appeased.
They are implacable as the law, thirsty for revenge.
Nothing will appease them but confession and punishment.

No one hears their condemnations save
those who cannot stop hearing them.

Clockwork Orange at Haydn University

Two paunchy men stood on the lawn beside the Class of '73 sign, delighted to have found each other. Their wives had gone to the benches to sit with other men's wives.

"Remember the Occupation?"

"Hull Hall? Of course I do. It was great, those two nights in the corridor outside the Chancellor's Office. Weed and making out."

"Their old house is gone now. I checked. Do you remember when Sigma got tossed off campus?"

"Yep. 'Hosting lewd and unnatural acts.' Wasn't it something like that?"

"That was the charge all right. They hung a sheet out the windows. Remember?"

"'Sigma died for your sins.'"

Suddenly, music blasted from the two loudspeakers on the east and west sides of the quadrangle. It was "Dear Bertolt," starting with the familiar drum riff from H.T., then the Hogans' clashing guitars, not one of the band's big hits, but a favorite with the SDSers, the anti-war radicals, with those who could quote Frantz Fanon, Angela Davis and Kate Millet, the ones who disdained cowboys, extolled Indians, immolated their brassieres and draft cards, sampled the whole pharmacopeia, raised fists, and had deferments. Then, in the fullness of time, they cooled off, lost hair, put on weight, got jobs, spouses, children, IRAs, high blood pressure, and life insurance.

A few of those in the Quad who were old enough smiled, recalled snatches of the lyrics, and sang along. More just joined in the refrain with sincere nostalgia, overlaid with embarrassment and self-mockery.

Those invisible lines they're red

To the Feds we might as well be dead

New Deal's same as the old Deal

You lie down and we'll make your bed

Yeah, it's obvious who lost who won

Yeah Yeah

What's robbing a bank beside founding one

Bunching together, they waited for the line, then shouted it out like a trained chorus. They all loved the band, loved themselves for still loving it, or at least the selves who used to love it.

No mortgage for the likes of you, son

A loan, are you being funny

We use bookkeeping you use a gun

Hand over your rainy-day money

For us the whole year is sunny

You're finished we're never done

Yeah Yeah

What's robbing a bank beside founding one

For the University's First Annual Alumni Weekend, the campus was spruced up with azaleas, ranks of tulips and daffodils, mown lawns, and fresh paint. The forecast for the last weekend in April called for ideal weather, warm and windless, perfect for the outdoor events. From noon to two, alumni and students strolled the campus where booths offered six varieties of ethnic food, baguettes, pastries, both Texas- and Kansas City-style barbecue, costly wines, cheap beers. Under the oldest tree on campus, a huge sycamore, there was a booth painted in bright psychedelic swirls selling newly legalized marijuana. When this daring move was announced at a faculty meeting, one waggish assistant professor whispered to another, "Recreational for the students, medical for the alumni."

Parents Weekend—for sociological reasons retitled Friends and Family Weekend—had been back in October, built around the familiar ceremonies of falling leaves, a football game, a pops concert, featuring unchallenging faculty talks on topics like "Dragons in Popular Literature and Film," "Six Ways AI Is Going to Change Your Life," and "How Teddy Roosevelt Saved Football." The springtime Alumni Weekend was one of the innovations of the University's recently installed President, Kevin Yoshimoto, who was so often called "a breath of fresh air" that the phrase might almost have been part of his title. Yoshimoto was just thirty-nine and held doctorates in both chemical engineering and American Studies. He had published two books, dozens of articles, and had delivered papers at conferences all over the globe. After reluctantly agreeing to a stint as acting provost at his old university, he found he relished administration more than research, even more than teaching. His wife liked it too. It meant less travel and more attention paid to her and their daughter. It also came with an administrator's salary. When Haydn announced that it would be searching for a new president, they agreed he should apply.

Yoshimoto liked being out of the office, being seen around campus. He would drop by departments and chat with the secretaries, sit in on classes, answer greetings and queries from students. He favored slim-cut jeans, blue chambray shirts, and old corduroy sport jackets, one black and a brown one with leather elbow patches.

Yoshimoto had the idea of an Alumni Weekend focused on the rock band Clockwork Orange not just because he was a fan of the classic group. Over the summer before assuming his post, he read up on Haydn, its policies, distinguished alumni, its trustees, and the school's history. He discovered the band's connection to the University in a yellowing copy of the old student paper that had died with the 70s, *The Haydn Free Chronicle*, known to students of the era as *The Freak*, and the idea sprang full-grown from his brow. He envisioned scholarly seminars with papers to be published in a new journal, *Clockwork Studies*, honorary degrees awarded to the band members, and music performed by a tribute band. Done right, he figured the Alumni Weekend could be a boost to fund-raising, which he was reminded over and over was any university president's chief function and top priority.

In 1970, George Slavitsky, Slav, enrolled as a freshman in Haydn University. He was tight with two fraternal twins from high school, Harry and Billy Hogan. In tenth grade the brothers had formed a band with Joe Belfiglio, who owned a bass, and Bob Rosenthal, who owned a set of drums. Belfiglio dropped out when his family moved away and Slav took his place. They called themselves The Hogans and, the next year, changed their name to The Hooligans. They played at two high school dances but mostly for themselves in the Slavitsky family garage. Rosenthal, a barely adequate drummer, was studious and smart. He got into Yale. The Hogans were smart but not studious at all. They didn't want to go to college and their parents urged them to do so only half-heartedly. "At least learn a trade," pleaded Mr. Hogan. "We've already got one," Billy retorted with a confident grin. What the brothers wanted was to be rock stars, to sing like the Everlys and live like the Stones.

Slavitsky signed up for a triple in Haydn's dorms then invited the Hogans to move in. Driving Slav's roommates out was quick and easy. Now they had a place to practice, a cafeteria to defraud, and a ready-made audience. But they were shy a drummer.

When Google informed him that there was just a single surviving member of Clockwork Orange, President Yoshimoto was saddened and disappointed, but not deterred. He summoned his hyper-efficient administrative assistant, Dami Awao, a young woman whose gast, he had learned, could never be flabbered.

“I want you to track down Howard Thurman Washington. He was the drummer for the 70s rock band Clockwork Orange.”

Dami gave her customary mock salute. “Aye, aye, sir.”

She was back in under fifteen minutes. “Like the band’s bassist, George B. Slavitsky, Howard Thurman Washington was enrolled here in Haydn. Unlike Slavitsky, he actually went to classes. He was on the Dean’s List all six semesters with a 3.9 GPA. His major was Cultural Anthropology. Instead of a minor he took a slew of electives—Anglo-Saxon literature to Zoology, you name it.”

“*Six* semesters? Did he finish early?”

Dami looked up from her notes. “He left at the end of his junior year.”

“Go on.”

“The band and their fans called him H.T. He was the oldest of the group and, according to four sources, the brains of the outfit. Also, as you must know, he’s also the only black.”

“Tell me something I don’t know. Like where he is now.”

“That took a bit of searching. Seems he’s become a Buddhist monk. Goes by the name of Hanshan.” Dami consulted her notepad. “It means ‘cold mountain.’”

“Can we contact him? He’s not in Japan, is he?”

Dami consulted her notes. “Upstate New York.”

"Good. I think I can get him here."

"He's a *monk*," Dami said. "He lives in a *monastery*."

"So I'll make him an offer he can't refuse, a Buddhist one."

President Yoshimoto began his letter of invitation "*Namo Buddhaya*," said he was a devotee of Clockwork Orange, tendered his condolences on the deaths of Slav and the Hogans, wrote that he regretted the unfortunate action of the University in having them removed from campus, and declared that Haydn now wished not merely to acknowledge but to celebrate its connection to the band. He laid out his plans for a new tradition—an Alumni Weekend—and that the inaugural one would be devoted entirely to Clockwork Orange, including scholarly presentations.

"We also want to grant you the bachelor's degree toward which you were working so excellently. In fact, we would like to do better by conferring on you an honorary degree, Doctor of Humane Letters.

"I understand that you may be reluctant to leave the monastery even for a weekend, but I hope you'll come. It's not just on behalf of the University. I would be personally thrilled as a fan and immensely grateful as CEO of the place. We will, of course, provide first-class transportation and meals meeting your requirements. By the way, my mother was a Buddhist and a good cook. We will put you up in the best local hotel.

"Please come. I appeal to you in the words of His Holiness, the Dalai Lama: *Old friends pass away, new friends appear. It is just like the days. An old day passes, a new day appears. The important thing is to make it meaningful: a meaningful friend—or a meaningful day*."

He signed off "I can promise you a meaningful day. Your New Friend, Kevin Yoshimoto, President of Haydn University."

Eight days later the President received a reply, to his surprise by email.

"Very well, Mr. President. I'll come on condition that you put me up in the dorm room shared so briefly by my friends before Haydn called the cops to drag them out. If McIlhenny's still standing, it's Room 411." Hanshan signed off by also quoting the Dalai Lama: "*I am a simple Buddhist monk—no more, no less.*"

Whether the band found H.T. or he found them is a matter of useless speculation. It's better to say they found each other one September afternoon on the steps of Hoffman Memorial Library. Slav and the Hogans were performing before a crowd of students all of whom sported long hair, bell bottoms or ripped jeans, fringed vests or louses, and peace buttons—the undergraduate uniform of the time. Howard Thurman Washington stopped to listen. As if he weren't already sufficiently conspicuous on campus, he wore a dark suit, like dead Malcolm and dead Martin. He was one of only a dozen black students at Haydn, a fearsome debater, a study in restrained and channeled anger. He scared people when he was silent and usually silenced them when he spoke up in class. He loved, in no particular order: his parents, two sisters, grandmother, Aunt Denise, Miles Davis, Bill Evans, British rock, and Max Roach. At a time when eating a grape or drinking a Coke was a political act, when radicalism was chic and Black Power in vogue, he kept his politics mostly to himself.

H.T. had a way with words, also with rhythm. He listened to the band for a spell then sat down on the steps next to Slav, laid his brown briefcase on his lap, and proceeded to give the band what it was lacking.

The impromptu concert/rehearsal ended, the crowd dispersed, leaving behind a little applause and just short of four dollars in loose change. H.T. was about to leave when Harry stopped him.

"Hey, man, you want to join the band?"

Before H.T. could reply, a cautious Slav asked, "You ever play *real* drums?"

H.T. laid his briefcase aside, stood up, and laughed. "Better than you play that bass."

"You have a set?" asked Billy hopefully.

"Did until I sold it last week so to buy the meal plan."

Slav and the Hogans laid down their guitars and put their heads together.

"What if we managed to get you a set—used but functional?"

"Well, I suspect you could buy back my old one. The trust-fund sophomore who bought will probably be bored with his new toy by now."

H.T. skipped his next class. He had never cut a class before, but he figured it was okay since he would be missing music theory for music practice.

The Hogans and Slav pooled their money and bought back the drum set for a quarter of what H.T. sold it for. The rich sophomore's roommate said he couldn't thank them enough.

The tribute band, who called themselves Clockwork Apples—perhaps so as not to be compared too critically to the original—was good. Their performance was one of sincere emulation rather than opportunistic imitation. They played an hour-long set after lunch in the outdoor Holbein Amphitheater for which, kitted out with two large speakers, was ideal. The alumni loved it, many finding it an antidote to the ponderous scholarship they'd experienced earlier.

The seminars had been scheduled for the morning. Six humorless academics dissected the band's oeuvre, deploying Gallic post-structural theory, musical hermeneutics, contextualization both historical and biographical, digital and political analytics. One alum, taking in the crushingly titled “Playing in the Generation Gap: Clockwork Orange’s Oppositional Deconstruction of Positive Post-Adolescent Aristippian Hedonism,” turned to her husband and whispered, “Huge ugly hammer, pretty tiny nail.”

Clockwork Apple led off their concert with the band’s 1972 breakthrough hit, “All-Nighter,” then ran through “Brown Rice,” “Figment of Your Imagination,” and an extended, Grateful Dead-like version of “Long Trip Through Bea’s Paradise.” They wrapped up not with something upbeat or raucous but with a moving rendition of “Cowboy Song,” the band’s haunting take on country-and-western, featuring an uncannily faithful rendering of Billy Hogan’s heartbreaking solo.

I left in the morning
when the whole world looked new.
I closed the door softly
and I didn’t tell you.

I would love to have stayed,
though you won’t believe me.
Guess I thought I’d fail you
or that you’d deceive me.

The highway led nowhere,
except further from you.
The morning didn’t last
and the world wasn’t new.

The college kids seemed a little let down by this melancholy finale, but the alumni smiled knowingly either at each other or to themselves. One or two wiped away a tear, then all of them stood and cheered.

President Yoshimoto went personally to greet H.T. at the airport on Friday night. He bowed, addressed him as Hanshan, and in the limousine told him what was planned for the next day.

Yoshimoto couldn't help being taken aback by H.T.'s appearance. He looked so old; his head was shaved, but he stood upright, lean and, dignified. He did not resemble the monks Yoshimoto had seen when he took his newly widowed mother to visit Kyoto. This was not just because he had never seen a black Buddhist but because H.T. displayed none of the subdued placidity, courtesy, and modesty he expected of a monk. The President was disappointed when Hanshan declined to attend Saturday's concert or any of the seminars but took comfort from his guest of honor's pledge to come to the banquet on Sunday which would be followed by the formal conferring of his honorary degree.

"And you'll say a few words?"

"I will."

Howard Thurman Washington was as good a lyricist as he was a drummer. "Dear Bertolt" was the first song he wrote for the band. They liked it at once and even more when he explained the title. Their first paying gig was at La Bohème, one of the college town's three clubs. The new song went over well with the undergraduate radicals and post-graduate literati.

Being black, better dressed, and far smarter than the others, H.T. was quickly granted the authority of a democratic aristocrat.

One afternoon, after a dull rehearsal in the dorms, Slav said he thought the band needed a new name. "Something not so, like, Fifties. More with it."

Everybody looked to H.T. who, never one to miss a beat, said "Clockwork Orange."

"Where'd you get that?"

H.T. opened his briefcase and extracted a soiled paperback. "Kismet," he declared. "Picked up yesterday outside the library. Somebody must have dropped it." He held the book up for them to see.

"Cover looks like a poster for *The Wild One*."

"Oh, it's better than that."

"Better than *Brando*?"

"Yes."

"Cool name, but it's a book," said Harry. "The title's taken; I mean it's copyrighted."

H.T. gave Harry an indulgent look before going into his professorial mode, the one he had used to explain who Bertolt Brecht was, also when he told them about Sherman's Field Order 15, the Freedman's Bank, Robert Johnson, John Dowland, and Alban Berg.

"You can't copyright a title, Harry," he said.

"No?"

"You mean I could write *War and Peace*," said Slav jokingly, "or *Hamlet*?"

"Prince of Denmark, in five acts, if you want."

"Wow."

"That can't be," Billy objected.

H.T. sighed. "The Copyright *Act* doesn't explicitly rule out protection of titles; however, the Copyright *Office* Regulations plus a ton of case law equate titles with slogans. Slogans can't be copyrighted. So, you like Clockwork Orange or not?"

"Well, yeah."

"Sure."

Billy was unconvinced. "It's good, but I don't want to get sued."

The next day H.T. brought along a xerox of the Code of Federal Regulations, Title 37 – Patents, Trademarks, and Copyrights.

"By the way, band names can't be copyrighted either."

Anthony Burgess's novel *A Clockwork Orange* was published in 1962. The movie was released in 1971. When the band became famous in 1974, the film company filed suit against both them and their recording company for infringement claiming the movie's title as a protected trademark—like Bubble Wrap and Barbie. Papers were filed with the federal district and a preliminary hearing scheduled. The press picked up the story. Clockwork fans crowded the courtroom on the appointed day and cheered exultantly when Judge Rudolph Giamatti dismissed the case in fifteen minutes flat.

The ballroom was filled with large round tables covered in starched white tablecloths. A waitstaff of work-study students in white shirts, black vests and slacks, stood at ease against the walls, hands clasped behind their backs. When President Yoshimoto, in full academic regalia, conducted H.T., dressed in his simple orange robe, to the head table, there were puzzled murmurs from the diners who were unaware that Howard Thurman Washington, the great H.T, had become the monk Hanshan. But, prompted by the standing ovation of those who did know, everybody rose and joined in.

The President seated himself on one side of the honoree and Susanne Shukovski, Director of Alumni Affairs and Development, on the other. Hers would be the name at the bottom of the solicitation letters, already prepared for mailing in a week.

Yoshimoto was served the prime rib, rare, Ms. Shukovski the lobster tails. Hanshan had the dish he had requested, beans, bok choy, and almonds over brown rice. To Ms. Shukovski's questions he replied politely but tersely and when she apologized for asking too many, he said, "Don't apologize. Ignorance is curable; it's stupidity that isn't." Yoshimoto asked if the food met with his approval. He nodded and listened indifferently to the President's account of the first time he had heard Clockwork Orange. "It was at a party. I think it must have been in middle school. It's your dinner made me think of it. The song was 'Brown Rice.'"

After the remains of the meal had been cleared away, President Yoshitomo asked Hanshan to accompany him to the podium. There was a lectern with Haydn's motto, *Lux et Veritas*, in gilded letters on the front and a microphone on top. The waitstaff withdrew discreetly and the crowd grew quiet.

"Dear alumni and guests, we are so pleased to welcome you to Haydn, mother of many souls. Our special guest is, as you know, the sole living member of a great and beloved band. Clockwork Orange got their start right here at Haydn and we are proud to have devoted this weekend to celebrating this enduring group of musicians. Life takes us all through many changes and our special guest is a distinguished example. When he enrolled here, he was Howard Thurman Washington, then he became the drummer H.T., and now he is Hanshan who calls himself a simple monk. As you may not know, he was among the brightest students Haydn has ever had. He would certainly have been elected to our chapter of Phi Beta Kappa and have graduated with highest honors. But he left us in his third year. I imagine becoming a rock star was a good deal more alluring even than graduating *summa cum laude*. We are here this evening for the University to make good the lack of his degree."

Yoshimoto turned to the left and a minion strode quickly to the dais holding a large, framed diploma. The President took it from him.

"So first, with genuine pride, I hereby present him with this diploma, mark of his much-delayed bachelor's degree." Yoshimoto handed the framed document to Hanshan who, not knowing what to do with the thing, put it on the floor.

"And now, a second degree. By the power invested in me by—and with the unanimous and enthusiastic approval of—Hayden's distinguished Board of Trustees, I hereby confer on him the degree of Doctor of Humane Letters, *honoris causa*."

The President nodded and the minion returned holding a doctoral hood folded across extended arms. The President took it and moved to lay it over the monk's bald head, but Hanshan held up his hand. He took the thing from Yoshimoto and dropped it on top of the diploma.

Concealing his exasperation, the President said, "Hanshan? Would you now say a few words?" and stepped back from the microphone.

H.T. took his place and looked out over the room for thirty long seconds before speaking.

"Thank you, President Yoshimoto for the degrees and the hospitality. Thank you, Trustees. Thank you all. I know it is not for me you've come but Clockwork Orange. I liked those white boys—Harry, Billy, Slav—liked their foolishness, their joy, their innocent delight in adulation and groupies. I even liked their sullen moods, fights, and vanity. They stayed children to the day they died.

"But, as for me, as you see, I have changed. I became good at renunciation—my anger, then my ambition, women, intimacy, writing, and, finally, the world against which nobody ever wins. I am grateful and I don't wish to offend, but I am standing here feeling unsettled, disturbed, and false. I shouldn't have come. It would have been wiser to stay where I was. Why? Here is the explanation. It is a poem by the sixth-century master Chen Hsi-wei, verses I might once have stupidly tried to set to music.

Lake Weishan lies cool and still as a forgotten bowl of tea,
the moon immobile as a yellow disk embroidered
on a gown of black silk heavy with pearls.

As time is change, so these motionless bamboo leaves,
these reeds standing to attention like proud veterans,
yield a moment without war, decay, turmoil, or age.

I too am still in this moment, captivated by
the moonlight on the enchanted lake, silver and gold.
The moon's radiance on the water looks so precious,
I reach out to touch it and so, with my foolish hand,
spoil eternal peace.
Alas! If only I had refrained."

There was a drawn-out silence, uncertain ripples of applause. President Yoshimoto stepped forward, seized the monk's hand and shook it twice, then he gave a deep nod aimed at the back of the room. The original recording of "All-Nighter," the band's ever-popular and infectious party song, blew through the ballroom as the black-vested work-study students hurried to push back the tables so the alumni could dance.

One-Hit Wonder

Does anybody think about Benjamin Schaber and his brief career these days? Is he quite forgotten? I forgot him but began thinking of him while reading the memoir of an aging member of his generation. The author doesn't mention Schaber, even in one of his many lists of names meant to evoke nostalgia. So, even a book devoted to remembering forgets him.

It was with Schaber as Scott Fitzgerald predicted it would be with him: the debutantes made him famous overnight. The publishers of *Thirty-Three Stories* played up the "voice of his generation" angle, but Schaber's aficionados weren't flappers bobbing their hair, raising their skirts, and guzzling gin. They weren't even the politicized young, wearing jeans with holes at the knees, fringed vests, hair as long as they could grow it. Not really. Schaber's real fans were, I think, disaffected and thoughtful young people bored by the stultifying 50s but embarrassed by the naïve zealotry of their contemporaries, the simplicities of the so-called Counter-Culture. They were like people stranded on a dwindling ice floe, the times eating away the middle ground beneath their feet. Between 1964 and 1969 there was war, riot, assassination, protest, insurrection, astonishing rock albums—many every month, it seemed. They simply became invisible. Such people do not make history. They don't want to. Schaber's fans were an invisible minority. As I imagine them, they mistrusted history. Where others see a decade—particularly the one in which they come of age—as distinct from all others, the fans of Schaber would have scorned such notions. The memoirist might have been a reader of Schaber as he grudgingly concludes of his college years, "Even the 60s weren't *The Sixties*." You can almost hear the condescending "My dear."

Why did Schaber's writing attract lukewarm young believers in a fixed human condition, bearers of the tragic sense of life and also the comic? As I see it, those who were so enthusiastic about Schaber were not optimists. Yet their very horror of optimism proves it must have been for them a powerful temptation. After all, they were for the most part young Americans, like Schaber himself. Optimism is Americans' default position, which is why we are so cherished and ridiculed by older nations. Schaber's most faithful readers longed for the sweetness of resignation; they preferred the inspiring, nebulous lectures of Buddhism's popularizers to the precise, lifeless ones in their required courses. Consider which of his stories was anthologized in the early 70s, included in the kind that printed rock lyrics side by side with real poems to for English departments anxious to appeal to rock-loving, poetry-scorning post-adolescents. "One With Everything" is the ambiguous title of Schaber's most read tale, a story so much of its time that it couldn't possibly outlast it.

One of my old professors, an apodictic formalist, declared that in a short story what counts is what happens, not to whom. This is not always true; some stories are plotless character studies, such as Schaber's "The Norwegian Suitor," "Me and Me Old Bamboo," and "Elvis Takes Tel Aviv." However, "One With Everything" perfectly exemplifies the professor's dictum; to whom the thing happens is the whole point. The protagonist of the story resembles historical personages (two of them, in fact) but is not quite either; Schaber uses no names, only official titles. Like Kafka's Officer, Land Surveyor, and Country Doctor, in Schaber's stories people's identities are sometimes swallowed up by their professions, especially jobs they detest, and so appear to be more processes or techniques than people.

So, "One With Everything." On a Thursday in April, shortly before lunch, the President of the United States takes a break from his many burdens. He walks out of the Oval Office, weaves his way through the West Wing, barely acknowledging all the secretaries and officials who leap to their feet; then he marches slowly upstairs to the residence which is empty, his wife and daughters being out. It is flooded with the soft sunlight of cherry blossom time. He meanders into his daughters' rooms. (It is, of course, significant that there should be two daughters; both Johnson and Nixon were the fathers of a brace of grown daughters.) The President rather brutally contrasts his daughters to one another, as if by schematizing them he were making fun of the deplorable polarization besetting the country. The younger daughter is still in college, a blonde, liberal-to-radical, drinks Pepsi-Cola with rum, isn't punctilious about shaving her legs and under her arms, prefers the Stones to the Beatles, smokes marijuana, lost her virginity at fifteen, is majoring in Urban Studies, and since she was eleven has thought her father wrong about everything. The elder daughter, a brunette, graduated the year before from a college without an Urban Studies department, is engaged to marry a West Point graduate, drinks lots of Diet Coca-Cola, never misses church, adores her father and is hygienically impeccable. Her room is so neat it looks to her father as if she has tidied it up preparatory to abandoning him for a decorous married life. The younger daughter's room is as disorderly as her life. In the doorway the President sniffs; to him the room smells of sex. (Think of Hamlet's "enseamed sheets"). He imagines all kinds of musky effluvia. On the floor, among the discarded undergarments, shoes and blue jeans, lies a book, just where she must have let it drop, spine up ("like my daughter?" he wonders). The book has a black and white cover, like all New Directions paperbacks, including those by the gifted traitor Ezra Pound ("Nude Erections, New York" is how the poet addressed his epistles to his publishers). The book his daughter dropped is *Siddhartha* by Hermann Hesse, a bestseller among the young, irresistible to the counter-culturalists who reckoned that if the foolish war in Vietnam is where middle-aged white businessmen led them then they'd prefer Indians, Asians, African-Americans, and women. *Siddhartha* and Journey *to the East* persuaded a lot of young Occidentals to dabble in Buddhism. Schaber seems to have dabbled too, though he may have been kidding some of the time.

The President looks idly at the statue of the Buddha on the cover. "Chubby and mongoloid" is how he registers the figure. This makes him think of Chairman Mao and so still more weighed down by the cares of his office, wearier. With a sigh the President lies down on his younger daughter's deranged ("defiled?" he wonders) bed. *Siddhartha* is still in his hand simply because he has neglected to drop it. He begins to read.

No one fails to note the sudden alteration in the Leader of the Free World and almost everyone is alarmed by it, including his long-suffering, oft-betrayed wife, who long ago made her peace with his ambitions, appetites, and oppressive physicality and feels frightened by this soft-spoken, kindly, transmogrified hubby who no longer tells smutty jokes and, in fact, has begun to sound saintly. The Cabinet members whisper among themselves and discreetly call in the National Security Advisor and the Director of the CIA. The President's military advisors grimace even more stoically in public and swear even more lewdly in private.

The President asks the networks for an hour of prime-time and addresses the nation. "My fellow Americans," he begins as usual, then adds, "my fellow human beings."

"What the—?" is heard in living rooms all over the country.

He declares an end to the war. An immediate end. "What the—?"

He lays out a new tax policy which might have been conceived by Robin Hood. ("What the—?") He hints at new appointments and coming initiatives, such as a huge rise in foreign aid. Westerner though he is, he then speaks about the deleterious effects of meat-eating, tobacco-smoking, and bourbon-drinking. It doesn't stop there. He deplores the internal combustion engine: "If there were any intelligent aliens looking down from their saucers, they could be excused for concluding that the automobile's our planet's dominant life-form."

The blonde daughter listens to the speech in a dormitory room, on a disheveled bed, wearing nothing but a pair of pink panties, lying close beside a bearded English major who is wearing nothing at all.

"Right on! This is great!" says the English major.

She begins to weep.

"Hey, what the hell are you crying about?" says the boy.

She rolls away from him and with the back of her hand she brushes hair and tears from her eyes. "Because they'll kill him, moron."

The end.

If I were pressed to formulate Schaber's position in a single sentence —where he stands, from which he writes—I would reply that his work is about the necessity to try and change the human condition and the impossibility of doing so. Given the chance I would add that, for Schaber and his most sympathetic readers, this *is*, in effect, the human condition. Schaber is a bit like that old Talmudist Rabbi Tarfon who wrote, "It is not your job to finish the task, but you aren't free to give it up either." Says Estragon in *Waiting for Godot*. "I can't go on like this" and Vladimir famously snaps back, "That's what you think." A less pious version, played as a duet.

For me, the quintessential iteration of this theme is the shortest of Schaber's tales, a monologue of only 224 words, so short that it merited a single letter for a title. This piece is hardly known at all because Schaber wrote it before *Thirty-Three Stories*, in which it is not included. The piece was published in an obscure and long defunct journal aptly named *Lethe*. I secured a copy of this journal; these days you can find nearly anything online, maybe even the lost books of Tacitus. Here is the complete story.

Z

"We tried to cross at two a.m. with this load of girls. We were all at the front of the truck, the girls, of course, stuffed in the back, nicely locked up. X. drove, Y. sat in the middle, and I rode shotgun. Of course, we all had guns. About a kilometer from the border Y. just went crazy. I don't know how he did it, but he managed to lift his foot over X's leg and jam it down on the brake. We nearly rolled over. There were screams from the girls, not all of whom are unaware of where we're taking them, by the way. X. cursed Y. and Y. cursed X. I kept my mouth shut. They took their argument outside the truck. It swelled up quickly, their argument, bursting out in all kinds of profound sociological, economic, historical, and even theological issues—very crudely stated, you understand—so that in the end I guess there wasn't any other way to resolve matters except by drawing their pistols. The girls, hearing the raised voices, fell as silent as myself. The two fatal shots, both to the head as luck would have it, made us all even quieter.

"Well, that's why I'm all alone with the load of semi-virgins. If you don't mind, I'll take their share. For their families, you understand."

The end.

"Z" is so cynical that it seems almost a kind of celebration of bleakness, the willing acknowledgment of a reprehensible truth and the world; yet simultaneously it is the most indignant of protests, an item, like those in Ivan Karamazov collected in his scrapbook, to throw in the face of the Creator of the Universe.

"I can't go on," said Y.

"That's what you think," says X.

So, who is Z? The author Schaber? What Schaber feared becoming if he were not an author?

Perhaps Schaber wrote "Z" only to prove to himself that he could. That's certainly possible, but I think otherwise. How often do writers astonish themselves—I mean with the unsuspected filth inside them?

When you actually meet authors, they are usually polite and almost studiously normal; quite a few come off as knowing and compassionate like the Buddha. The filth is kept private notwithstanding that it is published. I should think authors often take themselves by surprise, though, of course, readers must never suspect how the author's eyes grow wide while his pen, driven by forces outside his control, glides across the formerly pure paper.

Thirty-Three Stories came out in the Fall of 1970, excellent timing with respect to sales, reviews, acclaim. Public life seemed to have gone mad; a note of fatigue restraining the hype of 24-hour news stations, whose announcers sounded hoarse and exhausted from the intensity of recent years, too many big stories in too brief a time; it was beginning to feel like a wild party that had gotten stuck, needed to wind down but wouldn't. Apocalypse and utopia every couple of days. Woodstock and the invasion of Cambodia. Conventions turned into riots. Ghettos in flames. Students gunned down; leaders gunned down. The Pentagon descended upon, Catholic priests pulling break-ins. The Manson massacre and Lucy in the sky letting the sun shine in.

The author's photograph on the flap of *Thirty-Three Stories* merits semiotic analysis. In 1970 Schaber was twenty-six, good-looking and clean-shaven. The portrait is black and white, standard at the time and still deemed classier than color. The first thing you notice is where the photo was taken. Schaber is standing near the curb of a city street, behind him is a blur of traffic—a bus, cars speeding in opposite directions. The buildings across the street are likewise blurred, out of focus. Schaber is very much in focus, the focus, as though singled out from a blisteringly mutable environment. Because the blurring of space also suggests that of time, the picture intimates that he may be in his time but isn't of it. Then there is Schaber's hair, thick and dark with one curl falling Byronically all the way down to his right eyebrow. Its length is on the long side of the middle of the politico-cultural spectrum for male hair-length in 1970. In my opinion, were it much shorter or longer his book might still have been read, but by fewer people and perhaps understood differently. Not only do his locks resemble neither Richard Brautigan's hippie mane nor H. R. "Bob" Haldeman's Prussian crew cut, they are also not a precise *via media* between them. This was a time when wool meant one thing and gabardine something entirely else. You can see that Schaber has on jeans but, since he is under thirty, anything else would have seemed an affectation, "dressing up for the photo shoot." He is tieless, wearing what appears to be a Chambray work shirt with the two top buttons undone (*two*, not one). What unsettles the impression is that over this shirt he wears a dark suit jacket, manifestly well pressed. What does this jacket mean? Why not leather like Dylan or, for that matter, green Army surplus or even a rumple blazer? As for the expression on Schaber's face, I would call it illegible. The more you look at it the more contradictory it becomes—blank/intense, empty/intelligent, engaged/indifferent, fun-loving/ascetic. This photograph caught the public's fancy. It was reproduced alongside nearly every article about Schaber and, for some months, grew almost as familiar as Che Guevara's. This was the Voice of a Generation which, even the ersatz Monkees were singing to nodding pubescents, had *something to say*. . . a lot to say, in fact, though most of it neither articulate nor interesting. Schaber's portrait—candid/ posed—makes him look not only eloquent but anointed, an effect of the light which seems to seek him, pouring unction down between the skyscrapers.

As its title suggests *Thirty-Three Stories* has no obvious unity of character, setting, or theme. This is unusual in American letters. Publishers learned from Hawthorne and Poe, then from Hemingway and Fitzgerald, then from Faulkner and Salinger that story collections sell to the degree that they resemble novels; in fact, they will generally sell only if the author has already produced a celebrated novel. In this respect, the success of *Thirty-Three Stories* is unique. It was preceded by no well-received novel, and it appears to range pretty much at random all over the place.

Consider "Liebestod in Novosibirsk." The story opens in a morgue on a February night in the Siberian city on the Ob. Nothing works properly. Everything is ugly. Two policemen, cold and exasperated, deliver the latest stiff to Pyotr, our hero. Pyotr works the night shift, receiving and storing bodies as his father did before him. It is 1951 and Stalin is not yet dead. On the contrary.

The corpse is wrapped in a grey sheet retired from the local hospital; no point in wasting a blanket. The police know the drill and hurry through it, carrying the stretcher to the mortuary's one gurney, flipping the body neatly on to the steel surface. Pyotr bows deeply to the policemen, "as his great-grandfather did to the landowner, his grandfather to the Chekists, his father to the commissars." The policemen are not interested in searching out counter-revolutionary tendencies; they want only their receipt and to get back into their van where it is a little less cold. "Elsewhere cold is defined as the lack of heat," writes Schaber, "but in Siberia, in the winter, it's the other way around."

Pyotr's task is to strip the corpses if possible and lug their naked bodies on to one of the wooden shelves, tagging the right big toe with a serial number. It is not pleasant dealing with even frozen bodies, but Pyotr has become inured to the beaten-in faces, the discoloration, the stink of vodka and feces, the swelling, the blood. What he is entirely unprepared for is beauty. And beauty is what he sees when he removes the sheet. At the sight of her he staggers back two paces. The woman is young, in her early twenties at the outside. "She is already naked. No, she is nude. Pyotr has never before understood the meaning of this distinction," writes Schaber. This is the most beautiful thing he has ever seen in his life.

It is a sad story of necrophilia. Pyotr steals the corpse and hides it in a garden shed. Then he buys a used deep freezer and has it installed in the basement where he lives. He means to keep her in, to preserve her. Two hours before dawn on his night off he sneaks her in being as quiet as possible, terrified that his neighbors will hear.

Now that she is safely in the freezer, Pyotr talks to her, opening his heart as wide as anybody in Dostoyevsky. It is her stillness that makes her so beautiful, so receptive to him. He knows that if she were alive this woman would not look at him and also would not be so lovely. "There would be something displeasing about her voice, or she would use a coarse expression or impudently swing her hips. There would be something." But her perfect stillness makes her in his eyes perfect too. "He knows that she was probably a call girl strangled by some drunken customer and dumped in a snowdrift by the river—the marks of fingers are right there on her throat—but to Pyotr death has restored her virginity."

Pyotr goes on with his life, which was always solitary. People do not like to be around men who do his sort of work. He grows older and she doesn't change. Well, she does, of course, little by little, but Pyotr doesn't notice. "What is it like to be dead?" he asks her. She looks content with it. "Is it just nothingness? Is it like the same as not having been born?"

As spring approaches Pyotr resolves to kill himself. It is, after all, the only way to be with her. He decides to slit his wrists and takes his one knife to be sharpened for the purpose. He chooses a day, but when it comes, he puts it off. "What if death is something and not nothing? Something bad?" He kisses her frozen lips. He strokes her icy limbs. He makes some soup and decides to try again tomorrow.

And so it goes for an entire week: Pyotr screwing up his courage, hefting his knife, kissing her farewell—or hello—then losing his nerve. Finally, one morning when he returns from work, he cries to her, "That's it! Either I slit my wrists or I unplug the freezer. You use up so much electricity," he complains as if it were her fault and closes the freezer's top for the last time.

Pyotr rolls up both sleeves, takes the knife, and sits down in his easy chair. No, he can't do it. "Perhaps, he thinks bitterly, if I had a revolver, or one of those cyanide capsules, then I could do it."

Unable to kill himself Pyotr gets to his feet and disconnects the freezer "which shudders into silence like a dying ox." Then he collapses into his chair, puts his head in his hands, and cries. "He bawls so loudly that his neighbors overhead send their teenaged daughter Marenka to his door to find out what terrible thing has happened."

The end.

This is the kind of story that compels readers to ask why the author wrote it—not where he got the awful idea but why he persisted with it, imagining himself into such rank basements. Why Stalin's Russia? Why a pathetic and perverted Siberian mortuary worker? Why necrophilia? Was it to show that nothing human is alien to him, to make an exhibition of comprehensive empathy? A misplaced impulse to humanize the Cold-War enemy? Beauty is death, is stillness. Could it be a satire on aesthetics, on Wagner's overwrought Romanticism, the pornographic impulse to reduce women to things? Or is it the twisted fantasy of a sick author, a projection of his very own suicidal or sexual impulses?

No one can deny Schaber's collection has scope. But so do the steppes, so does the Sahara. Perhaps it was the sheer unexpectedness of each new story that made for the grandiose predictions about his future, the long, fulfilling career to which he and we could look forward. Still, it's possible that Schaber, young as he was, was like the magician who bows off the stage after performing every one of his half-dozen tricks, leaving the audience to believe he could do fifty more if he wanted.

It wasn't only the critics who anticipated this great future for Schaber. His fans were only too willing to adopt him as their voice, to idolize, even to apotheosize him. The craziest thought they saw in the number thirty-three a messianic hope—and said so, with disturbing sincerity.

The story I liked best when I first read Schaber's book was "Eine Kleine Sternmusik," his excursion into science fiction. I suppose I liked that it was at once implausible and persuasive, fantastic and quotidian. Here, as elsewhere, he walks a tightrope, acknowledging that life can be sticky or tedious and then depicting it as unreckonable, magical. Schaber declines to deny anything, implying that everything *could* change and that nothing *will* change. "Nothing makes me so pessimistic as optimism." I think Schaber would smile at Ionesco's dictum, smile and nod. But because he was, after all, a child of his time he might insist that hope is not the same thing as optimism because it doesn't skip the five hundred pages of suffering to get to the happy—but perfunctory and unconvincing—ending.

"Eine Kleine Sternmusik" is set in what was then the near future. Soviet cosmonauts and American astronauts return from their first joint mission to the moon. They have stayed for a full week. They return by the American method, splashing down, but the water in which they splash is that of the Black Sea—one of many clever compromises. The eight men are determined to be in good physical condition but will tell their debriefers nothing. They demand to meet privately with their countries' heads of state and refuse to appear in public until their demand is met. The world is clamoring to see the heroes, see them all together in open cars, emblems of global brotherhood and human progress. The space explorers are threatened but they are tough and stubborn.

The American president is secretly flown to the Crimea for a meeting at the Chairman's luxury dacha. The spacemen waste no time in getting to the point.

While they were on the moon they met with aliens, who established a base on the moon's dark side decades earlier. The leaders are momentarily stunned. "But it's not possible. You were monitored." "Not all the time, not all of us." As they recover themselves the leaders ask many such questions, the kind most readers would want answered.

The aliens aren't exactly ugly, but they don't look like us. Physical evolution is a process dictated by the environment and their planet differs from Earth, though of course not very much. Their bodies are symmetrical, and they have four limbs and two eyes; but everything is shaped differently. Because their planet's slightly smaller mass their adults are about the size of our twelve-year-olds. Like us, they have hair all over, but theirs has remained longer, fur-like, as their planet is colder than Earth by almost three degrees Centigrade.

Impatiently, the oldest cosmonaut addresses the leaders: "Your Excellencies, it isn't the differences that are remarkable. Quite the contrary." He goes on to say that while the physical evolution of life is variable—within certain parameters—it appears that mental and emotional evolution is not.

The leader of the American team explains. "They're pretty much just like us, Mr. President. Not inferior, not superior either. Better at space flight, obviously, and right smart at languages. But they couldn't get over our toilets."

And there is the cardinal idea of Schaber's story.

The aliens have their own political and economic disputes ("How could we avoid them?"). They haven't resolved their religious conflicts ("Not really resolvable, are they?"). They've produced poets, comedians, billionaires, day-care centers, insurance actuaries, undercover police, circuses. The aliens were initially astounded when they discovered we did too but then they realized it made sense ("Life is life.").

What they really admire about us is not our plumbing but our music. They are embarrassed to admit that this art has remained undeveloped among them, a matter of striking drums and gongs, altogether primitive. When one of their probes first picked up our musical broadcasts they were blown away. Our music is the reason they went to the colossal trouble and expense of building their lunar base.

The spacemen tell the leaders that they have a question and request to transmit from the aliens. They would like permission to visit but, being thoughtful creatures, they are anxious about the effect on our population. In the judgment of the President and the Chairman, would such a thing be destabilizing? Would it be good or bad?

A means of communication is easily found—a special radio frequency—and an agreement reached. A contingent of aliens will be allowed to visit but must do so in disguise. They will travel as a contingent of schoolchildren on tour: Russian kids in Canada, American ones in Egypt, French in China, Korean in Argentina, and so on.

Amid tight security the aliens land at Edwards Air Force Base in California. An itinerary is presented to them in accord with their wishes.

They will talk only of music. They deplore the breakup of the Beatles and are shocked that we no longer mourn the premature deaths of W. A. Mozart and Franz Schubert. They have their individual enthusiasms. One of them is crazy about Domenico Scarlatti, another Frank Zappa, a third loves the music of Sergei Prokofiev. Two are huge fans of Aretha Franklin and Bob Dylan and all of them adore Johann Sebastian Bach and Louis Armstrong.

With their chaperones, the aliens linger in jazz clubs, stand at rock concerts, fill seats at recitals at the Academy of Music and the Bolshoi; they get tickets to musicals on Broadway and in the West End, attend the Proms at Albert Hall. Though they love all our music, they are not undiscriminating. One of them, apparently a female, writes critical reviews under the pseudonym Viola da Gamba and submits them to local newspapers; three are published.

The few scientists who are in on the secret are dying to question the aliens about astrophysics and extra-terrestrial biology, but the aliens turn them down. The aliens also express no inclination to meet any political or military officials, nor do they wish to converse with our philosophers, writers, or religious leaders because, they say, these are likely to be more or less the same as their own.

Was there going to be a novel? Schaber's publisher promised one, announcing it with trills and flourishes. At first anticipation was keen. Then two autumn launch seasons passed without a novel from Schaber, or even a second book of stories. His publisher stopped talking about it. Watergate mesmerized everybody. American troops left Vietnam. OPEC cut off the oil. Inflation ballooned, also unemployment. Janis Joplin and Jimi Hendrix died. Jim Morrison and Cass Elliot died. Popular music's High Renaissance abruptly ended and its Mannerist phase set in. Bras were burned instead of draft cards. A million marriages dissolved.

No novel, never a novel. In 1974 Schaber published two more stories, quite short ones, neither in *The New Yorker*. As a writer he was clearly a sprinter, not a marathoner. After that—like an extinguished transmitter on a space probe, like an unplugged freezer, like an assassinated president—the Voice of His Generation went silent. *Thirty-Three Stories* has been out of print for thirty years. I have no specific information about what became of its author, only the general conviction that he chose an obscure and ordinary life. I hope it has been mostly happy, perhaps, by now, enriched by grandchildren.

March 5, 1953

The funeral was flowerless. Every early spring bloom had been expropriated by the KGB for their boss. Scarcely forty people dared show up. Charged with counter-revolutionary bourgeois tendencies, tormented and shunned by the Composers Union, his wife and sons held hostage in Siberia, he composed wretched anthems to power plants and worse, *Zdravitsa.* It was a case of write our *der'mo* or die. Nevertheless, masterworks of "anti-democratic formalism" continued to pour forth. His meager stipend was cut; he very nearly starved. Given another decade and he might have sluiced out all that filth with a flood of new symphonies, freshets of ballets; but the tyrant outlived him. A stroke felled him and then, only fifty minutes later, with surpassing irony, the other.

I like to imagine all those grief-stricken Muscovites in the grainy newsreels, ten deep on the ugly sidewalks, shedding their Russian tears for Sergei Prokofiev, only pretending to weep for Comrade Stalin. What could the secret police do, even if they were not deceived? They too would have feared for their jobs, their families, their lives. More purges or more liberty—either could spell ruin for them. Besides, some of those cunning thugs must also have loved *Romeo and Juliet*, been moved by the mighty *Fifth Symphony* or, at least, had children delighted by *Peter and the Wolf.* I'm told all Russians revered their high culture in those bleak days, the way only a people who murder their artists can. They say you could accost anybody on the Nevsky Prospekt and demand fifty lines of Pushkin without being once disappointed.

A dispute breaks out. *He brought us through the war*, cries a babushka. *He watched over everything, knew how many shoelaces to make, how many tanks. He was our father, our son, strict and vigilant. Whatever will we do now?* A bony man in an old greatcoat retorts: *Spare us your vigilant monsters. Listen. He went abroad yet returned. He experimented, composed whatever he wished; he could be by turns acerbic, savage, lyrical. He might have made a good life for himself in Paris, turned into Serge; yet he came back, back to us. And not just for our birches and mushrooms.*

Today, we listen rapt to the energetic *Third Piano Concerto*, marvel at the clever *Classical Symphony*, buy tickets for the latest incarnation of *Cinderella*. And, as we relish the buoyant *Flute Sonata*, composed just months before the bloody tide was turned at Stalingrad, we forget what lies on history's dust heap.

Falling

1. How We Met

“Oh God. I’m *so* sorry.”

“Sure.”

“And you insist you’re okay?”

“I’m fine. Really. The bike, not so much.”

“You’re not bleeding anywhere? Nothing’s starting to swell?”

“Nope. No gore, no swelling. Not my ankle, and not my ego either. I’m A-OK.”

“I can take you to the hospital. A clinic. Maybe you should have x-rays.”

“Entirely unnecessary. But it’s very good of you to offer me and the Trek a ride home.”

“The least I can do.”

“Oh, I can think of a lot less.”

“It was my fault.”

“I know you think so. But you shouldn’t.”

“But I should’ve—”

“So should I. Never mind. The mistake was mine. Besides, no offense, you’re too pretty to be to blame.”

“What?”

“I said you’re too pretty to blame.”

"What do you mean?"

"I think you know."

"Are you—are you *flirt*ing?"

"I don't know how to flirt."

"How old are you?"

"How old do you think?"

"Uh-uh. I'm not playing that game."

"Suggest another one, then."

"Geography?"

"Alcatraz."

"Zeeland."

"Is that in Holland?"

"There's one there, too."

"Too?"

"The one I was thinking of is in Michigan. Population just over five thousand."

"Are you *from* Michigan?"

"No, but I've been there."

"Where *are* you from?"

"How old are you?"

"I think this is where I came in."

"Okay. Let's talk about your biking."

"Oh, my biking. The thing that's brought us together."

"Unfortunately."

"Maybe. Anyway, there are days when I'm puffing uphill and worried my heart's going to protest too much, or once too often, or is going to attack me, and other times I daydream about my ideal bike route."

"What would that be?"

"It starts from my driveway and goes downhill for twenty miles until it arrives back at my driveway."

"That's impossible."

"Oh, I don't know. Maurits Cornelis Escher might have been able to design it. He was Dutch."

"From Zeeland?"

"For all I know. Holland, anyway. The Netherlands. A whole country devoted to biking. Know why?"

"Why?"

"Because it's flat, so flat that it's mostly below sea-level. It's not all downhill but pretty close. Better, in fact. With flat you get some aerobic benefit."

"Do you have some favorite routes that *aren't* all downhill?"

"I always take the same route."

"Sounds boring."

"Perhaps it is, but it could be why I'm still alive. I know all the potholes and risky spots. Safety first. It's worked well, for the most part. Not today, of course."

"I'm sorry."

"No need to keep saying so. Besides, I can see it in your face."

"I have a sorry face?"

"Very sorry."

"So. . . um, you always take the same route to be safe?"

"Right. And I assume everybody behind a wheel will kill me, if I give them half a chance."

"That seems a bit. . . harsh."

"Prudent."

"*Has* anybody tried to, you know—kill you?"

"A good ride is one during which nobody tries. I don't ride for speed but. . . prudently. . . for safety. There was a time when I hated being passed, even by twenty-year-olds in spandex shorts on top of five-pound racing bikes. No more. Prudence is the homely daughter of a bitter father."

"Who is? The father, I mean."

"Experience, of course."

"Ah. And now I've added another wrinkle."

"Not your fault."

"So you keep saying."

"You had the right of way."

"No, I didn't. I was coming out of the driveway, and you weren't."

"The laws of cycling prudence say that the right of way is determined by avoirdupois."

"Avoirdupois?"

"Your car weighs a lot more than my bike. Are you religious?"

"Pardon me?"

"You were coming out of St. Denise's parking lot."

"Oh. No. I mean, I was there to drop off some decorations for a wedding."

"You're getting married?"

"No. My friend Cecilia."

"Bridesmaid then? Maid of Honor? *Matron* of Honor?"

"Maid."

"Good. What do you do when not helping your friends get married?"

"I was just running an errand for Cecilia, not helping her get married."

"Point taken. And the rest of the time?"

"I'm a Chinese historian."

"You don't look Chinese."

"I teach Chinese history."

"That sounds like quite a challenge. Does it learn anything?"

"Are you always this annoying?"

"I can't help it. It's only about words. And I don't annoy just *any*body."

"Only strangers? Like me?"

"I don't know anybody like you."

"That's an odd thing to say. You don't know me."

"So, any particular *part* of Chinese history? There's a lot of it."

"Sui Dynasty. That's my specialty. It's the shortest. Only two emperors."

"Let me guess. A good one to begin it and a bad one to end it?"

"Never thought of it quite like that but, yes, that's more or less how it went."

"Who was good and who was bad?"

"Emperor Wen was hardly a lamb, but he was lot better than his son Yang. So yes, Wen was good, comparatively speaking, and Yang—his second son—was a tyrant, decadent, a ruthless drunk, warmonger, degenerate, spendthrift, and lecher—a nasty piece of work."

"How nasty?"

"I think he arranged the murder of his father."

"Really?"

"It's a matter of dispute."

"Cold case, eh?"

"Everybody detested Yangdi. His own generals finally got rid of him. Yet he's supposed to be one of the best poets of the Sui period. He was a monster, but he had his sensitive side."

"Really? Know any of his poems by heart?"

"He wrote this about peonies:

'Springtime radiance, gradually, gradually where does it go?

Again before a wine jar, we take up a goblet.

All day we've questioned the flowers, but the flowers do not speak.

For whom do they shed their petals and leaves, for whom do they bloom?'"

"That *is* rather touching. I'm impressed by your memory. Also, your fair-mindedness. Credit where it's due. I like the smell of peonies. Everybody does. But the bad emperor was right; they don't last long."

"Like so many things."

"Mayflies."

"Infancy."

"Summer romances."

"And honeymoons. Anyway, it just goes to show."

"Show what?"

"That not only isn't poetic talent caused by tuberculosis, but it's also no proof of virtue, either."

"Emperor Yang was also a critic. And, in his way, he was fair-minded too."

"In his way?"

"Someone showed him verses by two young poets. Yang judged them superior to his own, so he had them beheaded."

"Credit where it's due."

"Do *you* write poetry by any chance?"

"Why would you suspect me of that?"

"The way you play with words, or they play with you."

"Well, what can I say? At least I try my best not to."

"I don't think Emperor Yang Guang would have said the same."

"Here we are. On the left."

The physics of any event may appear simple; but the more closely you look, the more complicated the thing gets. For example, say you roll a yellow tennis ball down the dining room table. Friction and air resistance will slow it down some but, when it gets to the table's edge, it will fall off as if it is dying to make its way to the center of the Earth, loving that center at an accelerating a rate of 32 feet per second squared. But it won't get far, let alone to the center of the Earth. It will be baffled at once, hitting the floor (or dirt or grass or gravel) and bouncing to a height relative to a whole lot of what the experts airily call variables such as the height of the table, the temperature, humidity, and chemical make-up of the air, and whether the ball falls onto hardened cement or a shag rug.

Psychology can also appear simple and not be. For instance, suppose a ten-year-old boy wants to get a ten-year-old girl's attention and she has pigtails, so he grabs one of them and yanks it.

I met the love of my life because of physics and psychology. Optics had a lot to do with it, but I count optics as a branch of physics. Newton wrote a treatise that he titled *Opticks*, a significant contribution to knowledge, I'm told. Though I find it humiliating to admit, in the case under examination here, I think the physics (optics included) might be more complex than the psychology. Though I'm probably wrong—the mechanics of human brains being harder to calculate than the motions of yellow tennis balls—this is how I feel about it. From my limited and biased point of view, the psychology of our encounter was as simple as the physics of a mousetrap or a letter opener, and not all that different from either (snapping shut, cutting open). Like the tennis ball, I fell—first off my Trek, then for her. You may insist the second fall's one of life's mysteries, but I say it's simple, if you refrain from looking too hard.

The physics of our collision, on the other hand, I've never untangled to my satisfaction. She in her small Honda SUV coming out of Saint Denise's parking lot; me on my hybrid pedaling smoothly east on Hattersfield Street at 9:30 on a summer morning. Cloudless welkin. Stunning sunlight. I'm all the way on the right, in the bicycle lane, pedaling through the shade of a tall maple just as she's exiting the driveway of the parish church. She doesn't see me because of the shade, and I don't see her because of blinding July sunlight. When we *do* see what's going to happen, we both swerve to the right. My thigh brushes the Honda's fender, and my left pedal strikes its hubcap, and my arm knocks against her side mirror and the bike's front tire slips because of a rock and a moment of inattention. Then a tumble, squealing brakes, Trek's front wheel twisted, handlebars skewed, her face full of horror as I look up at it from St. Denise's freshly mown lawn and, for no sensible reason, start laughing. I'm fine, only the bike is damaged, along her equanimity, my resolute singleness, her delicate conscience, and my precarious dignity. She makes the offer of a ride and I accept. The twisted Trek fits in the back of her Honda so perfectly that the space and the bike might have been made for one another. I settle into the shotgun seat, put my hands on my knees. The Honda is tidy and gives nothing away. It smells of nothing at all, except, perhaps, for a faint whiff of myrrh. I keep glancing over at her profile, her hair, her hands on the steering wheel. And, through all the fifteen miles to my little house, we talk and talk.

2. What Happened Next

"Is there some place you've got to be?"

"Well, let's see. I've done my wedding errand and run down my daily quota of cyclists. So, it's the groceries next."

"Ah, the supermarket. Why is buying food less tedious than putting it away?"

"You're right. It *is* more tedious."

"It takes longer, so it shouldn't be. Look, it's nearly lunch time. Come in and I'll throw something together."

"Oh. I don't know."

"Afraid I'll poison you in revenge? Like some wannabe imperial usurper?"

"But you said it wasn't my fault."

"Just teasing. It's my way of dealing with the world which, like you, doesn't care for it."

"Well, what've you got?'

"Pardon?"

"To eat?"

"Hm. Canned soup, tuna fish, sourdough bread. There's homemade iced tea, and I'm pretty sure I've got a cake."

"What *kind* of cake?"

"A round one."

"Well, if it's *round*. . ."

She goes straight for the books, of which there are a lot. *Of making many books there is no end*, saith the preacher, and he saith it while making another book. He might have added there's no end once you start collecting the things either.

My classification puzzled and amused her.

"F. O. Matthieson, R. P. Blackmur, T. S. Eliot, G. B. Shaw, W. B. Yeats, E. L. Doctorow, I. F. Stone. . ?"

"Bet you figured out the organizing principle of that shelf."

"Kierkegaard, Conrad, Dostoyevsky, Chekhov, Gide, Szymborska, Kafka. . ?"

"Ones I re-read."

"Why so *many* books?"

"I used to be a scholar."

“Used to be? And what do you do now?”

“Make furniture.”

“Oh. So, you’re a craftsman with a good library.”

“You say that as if you approve of the combination.”

“Do *you*?”

“It was my childhood ambition.”

“Well, that accounts for the bookshelves being so nice.”

“Thank you. How about clam chowder?”

“Manhattan—or the real stuff?”

“You have to ask?”

“A whole shelf of Scott Fitzgerald and Nathanael West?”

“I was going to write a doctoral dissertation about them.”

“Going to?”

“Started. Didn’t finish.”

“Why not?”

“Let’s say I didn’t see eye-to-eye with my advisor.”

“Why didn’t you get a new one?”

“The English department didn’t work like that.”

“No?”

“If you’d fallen out with your advisor, could *you* have switched?”

“I’m not sure. My advisor was wonderful. Like a mother, really.”

“Mine was like a father, a father with a temper and a belt. I lost interest anyway.”

"And took up cabinet-making?"

"Bingo."

"What interested you about Fitzgerald and West?"

"It was a deductive interest."

"What do you mean?"

"I was interested in the downside of the Depression, the Thirties."

"There was an upside?"

"For the radicals, maybe. But I didn't care for the political stuff. So, I laid out my criteria and deduced which writers to write about."

"Fitzgerald and West."

"It's funny. When I started out, I thought the only link between them was the one in my mind. Then I kept finding more and more connections."

"Give me an example."

"West favored Continental writers. Fitzgerald was the only American he had a good word for."

"And?"

"Fitzgerald was asked to contribute to an article called something like 'The Best Unread Books of 1933.' He suggested *Miss Lonelyhearts*."

"That must have pleased West."

"*Miss Lonelyhearts* is a minor masterpiece that has a love triangle in it. West named the woman Daisy."

"As in Buchanan?"

"West had to parody everything he loved. He was like that."

"What do you mean?"

"One of those people compelled to make fun of the things they admire."

"Like you're teasing the world?"

"I wouldn't have said so. But now that you mention it, you might be right."

"So, did you find out any more? About Fitzgerald and West, I mean?"

"Oh yes. By the end of the decade, they both wound up in Hollywood. Fitzgerald was hired by MGM to work on prestige projects. He was unsuccessful. Meanwhile, West churned out B-movie scripts for a second-rate studio. RKO."

"Fitzgerald had higher standards?"

"You got it. Fitzgerald needed heroes to admire and, out in Hollywood, he picked Irving Thalberg. West didn't take the movies seriously, maybe just those who made them. Both of their last novels are about Hollywood. They were writing them at the same time. Fitzgerald hero-worshipping Thalberg and West ruthlessly probing Hollywood's rotten underbelly."

"Was there more?"

"Oh, yes. West died the day after Fitzgerald. They were both laid out in the same funeral parlor."

"What? Amazing coincidence!"

"Not a coincidence."

"Oh?"

"Causally connected."

"What was the connection?"

"The usual. Love and death."

"Tell me."

"Over the chowder. It's ready. I've got oyster crackers *and* Hungarian paprika. Authentic. From Szeged."

"Sweet or hot?"

"Sweet."

"Perfect."

I tried and failed to recall the last time anyone but myself had been in the house, so it was something to have *her* there, seated at my table, using the unused second chair. It was, in fact, the kind of gargantuan something that can blot out a gigantic nothing.

"Okay. Here's the story. West met Eileen McKenney in October 1939."

"Bike accident?"

"Dinner party. The accident came later."

"Uh-oh."

"A year before that party Eileen's sister Ruth published a book called *My Sister Eileen.* Bestseller."

"Wasn't that a movie? A comedy?"

"Two movies actually—a make and a remake."

"So, West and Eileen?"

"Jewish boy who changed his name and a Midwestern girl who changed her address. Both went West."

"Horrible pun."

"There's hardly any difference between a good pun and a bad one."

"If you say so. But back to West and Eileen at the dinner party. Was it love at first sight?"

"Guess so. They got married six months later, in April 1940."

"A happy ending. A comedy."

"If you could stop the movie there. Happy, but not an ending. They were both killed on December 22, the day after Fitzgerald's heart gave out. The Wests were on a hunting trip in Mexico when they got the news. Leapt in the station wagon and sped north for the funeral. Apparently, West was a reckless driver at the best of times. The crash was in El Centro."

"How old were they?"

"West was thirty-seven, Eileen ten years younger."

"That's so awful."

"Fitzgerald and West were laid out in the same funeral parlor. Pearce Brothers. There were substantial obituaries for Fitzgerald. West got a tiny notice. His first name was spelled wrong."

"Love and death."

"In that order. *Liebestod*."

"Makes me think of Yangdi and those two poets."

"Two dead writers?"

"Yes. And Eileen."

"Tell me why you believe Yang killed his father. I'd like to know."

"It's a matter of debate."

"So, some people don't think he did it?"

"Some respectable scholars. But I agree with the Chinese people who convicted Yang long ago. You could say it's become a traditional belief. The Chinese have a different take on history than we do."

"In what way?"

"We're always doubting the best stories. Debunking is a cottage industry for our historians. You know, like George Washington and the cherry tree. Jefferson and everybody being equal. The Chinese don't do that. On the contrary. Even though every new dynasty rewrote it, they like their history stable. Anyway, the Sui dynasty is fixed in their memory as if it all happened a couple weeks ago."

"But if the patricide's just a story, a popular legend, why do *you* believe it?"

"I don't think it's just a legend. There's circumstantial evidence. But even more, it's in character. Yang was the kind of man who'd kill two poets for writing well. He also got rid of his older brother. Ready for some round cake?"

"What kind is it?"

"Angel food, I think. You know, light and with a hole in the middle."

"El Centro."

"Ah. Who's punning now? Coffee?"

"Yes, please. So, what's the circumstantial evidence against the deplorable Yang?"

"For me, the best source is Sima Guang, a historian who wrote four centuries later."

"Four *centuries*?"

"The Chinese have a lot more history than we do. To them, four centuries don't amount to much. Small percentage."

"What's this Sima Guang have to say?"

"You're really interested?"

"I'm interested. Really."

"Okay, then. Wen had fewer concubines than any other emperor, only two."

"Faithful to his wife, was he? In his fashion?"

"Yes. I think he was, until she died. Anyway, according to Sima, while the Emperor Wen was vacationing at Renshou Palace, he fell ill. One of his two consorts left his bedside to answer a call of nature. Yang saw her and was overcome by lust and he molested her. She resisted and fled to the Emperor, who inquired why she was so distressed. Sima says she answered, quote, 'The Crown Prince was being indecent to me.' It's a good translation, 'being indecent' is a decent translation. 'Being indecent'. Very Chinese."

"Polite. Did the Emperor believe her?"

"He must have. Sima says he roared, 'Animal!'"

"So, he wasn't so sick that he couldn't roar."

"An important point, given what he said next which was, 'How can I hand over important affairs to him?'"

"Ah."

"Well, yes. Yang got wind of what his father said and sprang into action. He had orders forged replacing Wen's guards with his own. Renshou Palace was sealed off and Yang sent his chief deputy to the Emperor's bedchamber where he promptly expelled the eunuchs and the ladies of the court. Shortly after, Emperor Wen was found dead, his ribs crushed. As soon as he assumed the throne, Yang made his father's two concubines his."

"Poor things. What could they do?"

"Nothing, of course. Or, I suppose, commit suicide. But, as I say, scholars are still arguing. Milk? Sugar?"

"Just milk, please."

Love and death tend to shatter your plans. Love—or maybe just lust, that crude simulacrum—drove Yang to molest his father's consort, setting in train patricide, usurpation, a new corrupt regime, the snuffing out of one promising dynasty along with two talented poets. Love at first sight united the solitary West, our most pessimistic and unromantic novelist, with Eileen McKenney, the sunny Midwestern girl who might have achieved showbiz stardom if they'd never met, or if West hadn't given up a hunting trip for a funeral, three of them, as it turned out. West admired Fitzgerald and, after all, admiration is another form of love—the opposite of lust.

Odd that we'd have shared our scholarly obsessions over lunch, that I'd want to know all about the Sui emperors, that she'd be interested in the lives and deaths of two American writers from eighty years ago; yet no stranger than meeting because of a collision, our encounter outside a place where people get married. El Centro.

She complimented my bookcases. As for me, I was filled with gratitude to her Honda, the too-bright sun, the spreading maple tree.

3. Happily Ever After?

"Were Eileen and West happy?"

"I'm sure of it. West promised his agent that his next novel was going to be all sweetness and light."

"That's sad."

"So, is the wedding next Saturday? Cecilia's?"

"Yes."

"Have you got a dress and a date?"

"Got the awful gown. It's *peach.* I don't need a date. I'm a bridesmaid."

"Is that some sort of rule? Bridesmaids have to wear awful gowns and can't bring dates?"

"This one doesn't."

"Recent breakup by any chance?"

"Maybe. But look, it's getting late. Now, you're sure you're okay? Really?"

"Absolutely. Never better."

"Okay, then. Guess I should go. Supermarket beckons. Thanks for lunch and the chat."

"Why don't you stay?"

"Excuse me?"

"Stay."

"You mean for the whole afternoon?"

"We could talk more about Nathanael West and Eileen McKenney and the Emperors Wen and Yang."

"Are, you kidding?"

"We could have a nice dinner."

"Dinner?"

"Well sure, to begin with."

"What? You need a ride to the bike place or something?"

"Not really."

"Then, what? I'm not sure I follow."

"It's simple. I want you to stay."

"You're not going to pull a Yang, are you? I've got pepper spray."

"Look, here's an idea. What do you say we give it a year or two and see how it goes?"

I fell. I didn't fall because of sudden lust, like Yang's, nor was the collision that felled me lethal, like the Wests'. My fall was a fortunate one, a lucky accident. Perhaps I fell with the blessing of Saint Denise.

Happily ever after? Who can say? Ever after's a long time.

www.ingramcontent.com/pod-product-compliance
Lightning Source LLC
LaVergne TN
LVHW041032150826
845672LV00001B/280